PRAISE F
𝕹ightfall and 𝕻tt

Jacob Steven Mohr's *Nightfall and Oth*   assembles such a staggering array of authorial voices, forms, and frights that it reads like the worst nightmares of fifteen feverish brains all preserved together in a single ghastly jar. An impressive collection of experimental, classical, and personal horrors, *Nightfall and Other Dangers* is sure to satisfy readers of every taste. — Gordon B. White, author of *Rookfield*

The stories in *Nightfall and Other Dangers* are populated with people you know. They are your neighbors, your friends. They're you. Mohr deftly mines the familiar for not only terror but painful truths, reminding us again and again that there is no safety in the places and people we know. — J.A.W. McCarthy, author of *Sometimes We're Cruel and Other Stories*

Nightfall and Other Dangers is an old desk in a condemned house sprawled in bloodied parchment. You ask yourself how they all came to be here—these leaflets marinated in grief, weird, and wonder. But don't worry, Mohr's right behind you, and he's here to set the record straight. — Scott J. Moses, author of *Non-Practicing Cultist*

There is an artistry to Mohr's writing... His debut collection is deliciously varied and welcoming to readers of the gothic, slasher, speculative, weird and creepy... This is the kind of selection you can pick apart no matter your mood. It will serve you and your hell well. — Aiden Merchant, author of *Sickness is in Season*

JACOB STEVEN MOHR

Nightfall and other Dangers

JOURNALSTONE
YOUR LINK TO ARTIST TALENT

ISBN: 978-1-68510-084-1 (sc)
ISBN: 978-1-68510-085-8 (ebook)
Library of Congress Catalog Number: 2023933294

First printing edition: April 7, 2023
Published by JournalStone Publishing in the United States of America.
Cover Design and Layout: George C. Cotronis
Interior Illustrations: MB Henry
Edited by Sean Leonard
Proofreading and Interior Layout by Scarlett R. Algee

JournalStone Publishing
3205 Sassafras Trail
Carbondale, Illinois 62901

JournalStone books may be ordered through booksellers or by contacting:
JournalStone | www.journalstone.com

For Shaumya

Contents

Introduction

I first met Jacob when he was working as an editor for one of my previous publishers, and I remember being struck as much by his overwhelming positivity and enthusiasm as by his impressive editorial skill. Here was a young man, I thought (because Jacob is objectively young, or at least younger than me, but in a sort of slightly unsettling Dorian Gray kind of way, where his jaded wit and wisdom seem to belie the youthfulness of his appearance...as though perhaps he's an ancient being that is merely wearing that friendly visage for a time, until it ceases to suit his purposes), who can not only help ready my novel for release, but also make it the best goddamn cyberpunk book ever written!

I had pigeonholed Jacob as an energetic American marketing type of dude, affable and enthusiastic, likeable and polite, and good at blurbs and manuscript surgery. He left the publisher before the novel was released, which I was extremely sad about, because he had done a fantastic job with the edits as well as with the cover art and the trailer (this was a small indie publisher where jacks—and Jacobs—needed to ply multiple trades), but time passed, and the book was eventually released, and it earned enough critical acclaim for it to be something we can both be proud of. Life moved on, and the planet continued its great roulette-ball circuits.

But Jacob, I soon learned, was far from finished with me.

We had kept in touch via social media, and one day he asked me if I'd like to read his horror novel, which I think at that time had not yet been accepted by its eventual publisher. One thing you learn when you become a writer is that there is a huge and crushing obligation to read other writers' work; you're supposed to have a blog, write reviews, support fellow authors on your label, keep your finger on the pulse of the current hottest releases, critique the secretly penned drafts of your friends and family, and somehow also still fit in reading for actual pleasure, the activity whose enjoyment first led you down the bewildering path to attempting to write for a living in the first place. This constant deluge of *stuff to read*, some of which might charitably be called "in need of a bit of work," leads to the development of something of a mind callus, a sort of crusty rind that protects the brain from disappointment by deadening its ability to truly appreciate what it consumes. Good writing, bad writing, original writing, derivative writing...it all becomes a stale, watery gruel that you glug down whenever you have a spare moment, enjoying and remembering little. It's like becoming a chef and immediately having your taste buds cut out.

Then I read *The Unwelcome*, and remembered how much I enjoy great horror novels, and I realised that Jacob was not merely an energetic marketing type of dude at all. He was an extraordinarily talented writer, a master of slowly ratcheting terror, a shadowy puppeteer able to jerk human dreams and emotions like obedient marionettes. I won't dwell on that book except to insist that you buy it, and read it, and experience simultaneously a masterwork of elevated literary horror and a top-drawer, old school slasher movie.

Perhaps I also won't dwell on it because it unsettled me. Jacob's book, which I demolished in a handful of sittings, left me with a lingering coldness, like a shudder that still hasn't truly ended.

But most of all, I won't dwell on it because this is not an introduction to *The Unwelcome*, but instead an introduction to *Nightfall & Other Dangers*, Jacob's newest short horror fiction collection, a sinister spawn I am honoured but somewhat daunted to have been asked to write a foreword for. The feeling is a little like being handed a homemade blanket made from disturbing and unidentified skins and asked to stitch some small scrap of my own flesh to one end of it.

After devouring the book in a few days, and spending many more days reflecting on it, waiting for its haunting images to end their tenancy in my head, and for the chill to finally seep out of my bones (it hasn't yet), my grisly addendum is as follows.

Nightfall & Other Dangers is the best kind of book because it's a book of ideas. But unlike some anthologies, so bursting with innovation that reading them feels like being blasted in the face with a sawn-off shotgun, these are ideas that reach out to you in a much more insidious way. A seed of doubt planted next time you're spending time with friends in a remote place. A flicker of horror when you glance at a peculiar statue and wonder if its eyes are more alive than they ought to be. An icy kernel of dread that nags and gnaws at you while enjoying a hot summer's day at the beach.

This is not intended to be some sort of warning, or a trite "read it if you dare." This is a full-hearted recommendation for a collection of fantastically well-written stories. But it's one you should only take if you're happy for the temperature of your blood to drop—and take a long time to rise again. I'm afraid I can't yet tell you how long, exactly.

Jon Richter, April 2022
Author of *Rabbit Hole* and *The Warden*

Nightfall

and other

Dangers

Nostalgia

Growing up, my mother kept a garden of hands. Pale grasping hands on slender stalk wrists, reaching up from the soil in our backyard. The hands were not of a size; no two were alike at all. Some were scarred or had tattoos. Some were missing fingers. Some were smooth and whole. But they all stuck in the ground the same way, emerging where the elbow would bend on a normal arm. Palms open, they followed the sun, and their fists shut tight when night fell.

Then we had to move away from that house. When people came to look the property over, the garden of hands was already gone and paved over smooth. Not a speck of soil was out of place; no trace remained that our strange crop had ever grown there. I don't know what became of the hands. My mother, silent and dark and full of secrets, never spoke of them again. But now I'm grown and my thoughts will often fly back to that strange garden of my youth, to my mother's secret harvest of wrists and fingers.

And when people pass on the street, I watch what extends from their sleeves. And I wonder.

You Are the Hero of Legend

You are alone in these woods.

You are a small boy of seven or eight. You are walking between tall trees, somewhere in back of your house. You are not far from your own yard, no more than a few hundred feet off. You feel as though you have been walking for hours. You are exploring a vast unknown world of green and shadow. You are an adventurer, dispatched on some gallant quest. You will discover something soon. You are not afraid of it yet.

You brush through dense foliage, scratching your cheek. You put your hand to your face, seeing small dots of blood on your fingers. You see something else: something gleaming up ahead of you, over a rise. You forget about the cut on your face. You are curious about this gleaming thing. You climb the muddy rise to see what lies beyond.

You see the stone. You see the sword.

You slide down that short hill on your bottom. Your little heart beats hard inside you. You know this story—at least you know its parts. You understand that finding a sword, a sword lodged in a stone like this, is exciting for a small boy like you. You walk up reverently. You understand, too, that reverence will be important for what must come next. You don't notice how still the forest has become. You don't see how the light has changed around you. You see that long, nocked blade, the cross-handle grip. You stretch out your hand.

You stop suddenly, crouching down low. You notice the message carved into the base of the gray stone. You run your hand over moss-covered words. You read them slowly, written in this ancient dialect. You whisper them in a voice stretching beyond time:

"You can become the hero of legend."

You feel the sun on you now. You see light—brilliant glory pouring down through the trees. You see the light gleaming off the blade's steel. You reach out with both hands and grasp the hilt of the sword. You think of a prayer your mother taught you, moving your lips silently. You don't hear it when the air starts to hum with terrible energy around you. You pull.

You hear something, a low grating sound. You felt the sword move. You felt it slide, a small distance, but progress all the same. You pull again, with all your strength. You put your foot against the mossy rock and pull and pull. You think your hands will break. You feel like your arms will be plucked off your shoulders. You don't give up. You hear that sound again, the sweet noise of steel moving oh-so-slowly across stone. You shake sweat from your face.

You pull. You pull.

You feel something loosen and give—you stumble back a step. You watch the blade fly free and thud against the forest floor.

You are holding the sword in your hands.

You open your mouth, whooping suddenly at the sky. You make animal noises, jungle noises. The sounds you make are loud and wild and joyous. You feel the weight of the steel in your hands. You feel strength surging inside you. You open your mouth again...

You scream. You cannot stop screaming.

You feel it start in your arms first. You feel this tightness, stretching taut inside you. You feel something growing, something expanding. You feel it pushing out through your skin. Your skin is not large enough for the hero of legend. You feel muscles, not yours, burst out of your body all at once. You feel the pain everywhere, in every part of you. You feel like an exploding star. You feel like a pimple bursting between two fingernails.

You hear both legs break and stretch. Your bones are not long enough for the hero of legend. You cough. You watch blood spatter on the ground. You taste copper on your tongue as your jaws split open. Your mouth will soon contain every tooth belonging to the hero of legend. You are on your knees now. You still cannot let go of the sword. You feel its weight anchoring you. You feel this everywhere. You feel that weight, even through the pain. You break, again and again. You grow. You crack. You change.

You lie gasping on the forest floor. You see the sky through tree branches interwoven like fingers. You can barely feel anything now, only this new sun on your face. Your face is not your face at all. You know from school how many bones your face has. You feel them moving. You feel them sliding under your skin, shifting and tearing. You know, somehow, that you asked for this to happen. You're getting what you wanted.

You read, etched in stone beside your head: "You can become the hero of legend."

You bleed slow and hot into the dirt. You feel its wet warmth everywhere. You are grateful the agony is dulled. You try to steady each painful shuddering breath. You grasp the hilt of the sword, so cold now in your unyielding grip.

You will not let go. You will never give up that glory again.

Song of the Summer

It wasn't really summertime anymore. The three of them squinted at a colorless sky, the boys pulling on the oars. There was still some heat left in the air, but the sun was already dipping low, bloodying up the horizon. It was light enough that Cameron could see the other two behind him in the stern, rendered dim and shapeless under the sunset. In the distance, Cabot Island loomed up from the water like Poseidon, bearded by trees and green scrub.

Shanna screamed out "Dolphins!"—suddenly the boat rocked to the left as she leaned out, pointing, shielding her eyes with her other hand. Water splashed in, pooling cold at their feet. Cameron dropped his oar into the canoe-bottom and steadied himself. Sure enough: maybe sixty feet off, dark swells tipped by swept-back fins curved up from the water in a pleasing line. He let himself smile; Shanna slapped the water. "Think we could row out to them?"

Cameron hesitated—they'd been rowing twenty minutes already, and his arms felt like they were full of wet sand. The answer came from the back of the canoe: "Why not?" Hyde shrugged muscular shoulders and pulled hard on his own oar, bringing them back to course. "I bet they wouldn't even notice us. Evening's feeding time for dolphins. I read that somewhere."

"You getting this, Cam?" Shanna's grin, directed his way, was brilliant even in the twilight. "Look who cracked a textbook. Tell us about the *fishies*, why don'cha."

"You go on and laugh," came the easy reply. "Tell her, Marine Bio."

"It's true," Cameron said at last. "The fish they eat come out now, when the sun's low."

"You hear that?" Hyde leaned forward, baring his teeth with playful malice. "That's the dinner bell. *Da-dump, da-dump...* And not just for the dolphins..."

He drove his fingers suddenly under Shanna's ribs—she shrieked out, "Knock it *off*," but when he relented, she fell back against him in a fit of giggles. He looped an arm possessively around her, then let go and continued rowing, all talk of dolphins forgotten.

Cameron turned away, thrust his oar down into the water. Behind him, he heard Hyde talking low in Shanna's ear, not the words but only the bass rumble of his voice, followed by her high clear giggle. It was a private, intimate sound. The back of Cameron's neck burned; for a split second he wished he was somewhere else, anywhere else. He pulled hard on his oar until the sound of lapping water drowned the others out. Shanna's portable speaker raised up its voice: David Lee Roth told the world how he'd been to the *edge*, baby. In Cameron's pocket, the beads of the woven bracelet spelled out S-H-A-N-N-A in a rainbow of colors.

Hyde hummed again: "*Da-dump, da-dump...*" Shanna laughed and slapped his arm.

Ahead, the island rose and rose.

The beach was only a narrow strip of sand, running like a white ribbon around the whole of the island. In Cameron's memory it was a fairyland, green and dark and forbidden. Now it looked somehow smaller, as though the sea had risen up around it. They dragged the canoe ashore, unloading the tents and cooler before they hoisted the boat onto their shoulders and hauled it and the oars up into the beach-scrub, out of sight of the water. In the cooler was food for the morning to come, plus Captain Morgan and a half handle of Chairman's Reserve and a twelve-pack of something called Riptide. A good haul of treasure, pillaged from three dorm fridges—enough at least to keep three college juniors slickered the rest of the weekend.

Cameron watched Hyde shoulder a huge duffel up the beach. They'd all packed tents, but he figured it was five to one odds Shanna would wind up in Hyde's wigwam that night. The thought twisted inside him like a hook. She'd sat so close to the other boy the whole paddle over, kind of cuddled up against him, and Cameron had to admit they looked natural together. Now she was spread out on the picnic blanket on the white sand, too bright to look at straight on. All he could see was the girl who'd snuck onto his front porch on school nights all through high school—with a pizza or a gaming magazine or cigarettes she'd lifted from her big sister's purse. He called out to Hyde, and together they wandered down the beach gathering armfuls of driftwood for the bonfire, leaving Shanna basking.

"Hot *damn*—she's a firecracker," Hyde whispered to him once he figured they were far enough away. "How long did you say you've known her?"

"All my life, I guess." Cameron watched a crab scuttle away from his sneaker, toward the water. "We were sort of neighbors, before college. Our families knew each other."

"Hot *damn*," Hyde repeated, not really listening. "I owe you a big one."

They took turns with the hatchet, hacking dry gnarled logs down to size. Pretty soon they had enough for the fire, and all three of them were circled up on that narrow beach, pouring alcohol into their faces while gray smoke oozed up toward a hazy sky.

"Here's to one more lousy year," Hyde toasted, smiling. He clunked his bottle against Cameron's. Somewhere in the twilight, the last gull of the evening screamed.

Three, four, five beers in, all the empties lined up neatly against his legs. Shanna laughed at some dumb joke, and Cameron started feeling a little better. Riptide was an IPA with a lemony sun on the label. He picked at it with his fingernails, piling the shavings gingerly on the picnic blanket beside him. The portable speaker was in Shanna's lap; David Lee Roth switched over to The Beach Boys, and Mike Love asked them, *wouldn't it be nice* to be just a little older.

Cameron shuddered. The good feeling didn't last; it never did.

It wasn't really summertime anymore.

Now the air was cooling fast, and getting darker by the moment. They huddled closer to the fire. Hyde lounged with one arm propped like a kickstand in the sand, swigging straight from the rum now, his all-American good looks turned up full blast by the firelight. And Shanna, with her Misfits t-shirt on over her bikini, sat cross-legged next to Hyde, letting him put his huge arm across her slender shoulders, that left hand slipping lower and lower toward her breasts. Cameron was facing the water: a half-mile of dark ocean lay between Cabot Island and the mainland, and already lights were standing out against the dark stripe of land in the far distance. The wind moved languidly, tasting like salt. When the conversation lulled, there were no screaming gulls, only the gentle roar of surf and the crackle of dried driftwood in the fire.

Cameron drained his fifth—or was it his sixth? He was starting to wish he'd never told anybody about the island. The cooler air, the sight of Shanna curled into the crook of Hyde's arm, smiling blearily through the flames...it was forming into a pool of something cold and thick in the bottom of his stomach. It had been like this all through college. They'd be out at a party somewhere, him and Hyde, or anywhere. There'd be girls that hung off his roommate's neck like there was a blizzard roaring outside and he was a space-heater. Cameron could talk to girls just fine so long as talking was all he wanted. But there seemed to be some other language he couldn't speak, some secret sign. It always left him with that same uncomfortable feeling deep inside of himself, the feeling that the whole world was turning at a speed he couldn't keep pace with, that it would leave him behind someday.

He didn't hate Hyde—really, he was grateful the other boy decided to drag him around on the weekend, to games and parties and shows, even if he did hate noise and smoke and the way strangers stood too close to you when they talked to you. He was willing to admit to himself that Hyde was probably the only real friend he had, excepting Shanna. But sometimes that cold miserable feeling made him wish the other boy would get a tapeworm.

It didn't make him feel any better, wishing that. But he wished it all the same.

Hyde tossed his long hair out of his eyes and slicked it back, tucking it all under a baseball cap. "You all right over there, Marine Bio?" He leaned across the fire and waggled the last of the Chairman's Reserve under Cameron's nose. "Wash the taste of blues out of your mouth," he said in a flattened kind of voice.

"I'm all right." He took the rum, pretended to drink. Shanna caught his eye across the blaze—some expression he couldn't quite name. He felt a bizarre thrill run through him, and he set the handle down in the sand, making sure it was steady and wouldn't spill.

"You're too quiet," Hyde pressed. "You're spookin' me."

"Cam's mysterious," Shanna intoned. "It drives the girls wild."

"Is that right?" Hyde leaned forward again—his grin looked like it might slide off at any minute. "For real...he brings us all the way out here, and he sits there not talking."

Cameron shrugged. "I've got nothing to talk about, I guess." His tongue felt thick and slow, like it belonged to somebody else, some dead slow thing.

"It's creepy is what I'm saying," Hyde said.

Shanna nodded: "*Creepy* and *kooky* and altogether *ooky*."

"I'm all right," Cameron repeated. But that cold black feeling turned inside him. *Why don't you leave me alone?* it screamed inside his head. *Why can't you ever just leave me alone?* The bracelet in his back pocket burned like a metal brand against his skin—around the other side of the fire, Hyde leaned down to talk close in Shanna's ear again. And again Cameron heard that low secret rumble, that private for-your-ears-only sound. Hyde's hand was slipping even lower now, around her shoulders, the fingertips actually kissing the swell under Shanna's t-shirt...

Cameron had to repeat himself twice. He said: "I know a story about this place."

Shanna leaned forward, interested, shrugging out of Hyde's grasp. The other boy let his hand drop without protest. "The dead speak!" he said. But he seemed stuck there somehow, unsure how to proceed. His mouth hung a little open, and he only shut it when Shanna asked:

"Is it a *ghost* story?" She switched off the speaker in her lap. "I love ghost stories."

Cameron shook his head, feeling his brain swim a little. "It's not a ghost story," he replied, a little uneasily. "But you said I was spooking you. This is the spookiest story I know."

Their eyes settled on him; he squirmed, suddenly completely miserable. But he started talking, haltingly at first, unused to storytelling. But after a while the words poured out of him. He didn't know where the story came from at all, and by the time it was done with him he felt breathless, as though he'd just run the eight hundred—like the telling had taken something from him, fed off him. He started out with the truth. Where he ended up, nobody could answer.

"I've...been coming out to Cabot Island since I was a little kid," he said. "But this happened even before that, before I was even born. My Uncle Jonah told it to me—you met him once, Shanna, at that picnic when we were still at Burr Banks. He used to come out here when he was a kid too, back in the seventies. And that's when it happened."

"*The murders...*" Hyde rumbled. Cameron ignored him.

"Uncle Jonah had this group of friends in college—three or four of them, I don't remember exactly. But they all came out to Cabot sometime around the end of summer, on a night like this. Uncle Jonah had the flu and couldn't go, but the rest of them came out and before they made camp they thought they'd walk along the beach a little. They were younger than us, just kids really. They wanted to get one last jolt of summertime before they got locked down by classwork. And after they'd been walking a while, one of them trips over something in the surf—a huge conch, washed up on the beach only a few hundred feet from this spot. That's when everything started going wrong for them."

He paused, groping on the ground for the Chairman's. He was sobering up quick, and suddenly he didn't want to be sober. Shanna raised an eyebrow. "A conch—like the seashell?"

"Like *Lord of the Flies*." Cameron nodded. "Uncle Jonah showed me a picture of the kind he thought it was...with spines all down the back of it. It was bigger than two fists put together, like this..." He held up his own hands. "So they take it back to camp, and they start in doing what we're doing right now. Drinking, listening to music. Teenager stuff. Then one of them gets the idea to listen to the conch, you know, to hear the ocean. So he listens..."

He paused again, hesitating. The end of the story had just struck him, but as he looked across the fire at the two pairs of eyes staring into him, the urge to stop talking altogether overwhelmed him. A funny feeling prickled down his neck and down the backs of his arms...it wasn't the anxious cold feeling he'd felt earlier, the one that came without a cause. This was something else. The start of something—a slow shift, a change in the air...

"What did he hear?" Shanna asked impatiently.

"Uncle Jonah didn't know," Cameron heard himself say, as if his voice was coming from a different room in a house. "Nobody knows what it was. Maybe it really was just the ocean, like he thought it would be. Maybe he didn't hear anything. But he put the conch up against his ear and the others saw him go kind of slack, kind of spaced out. He was definitely listening to *something*, even if there was nothing to listen to. And he had an axe with him..."

He wiped sweat off his forehead, scooted back from the fire, wiped his forehead again.

"He had an axe with him. And all throughout, his face stayed completely slack, completely empty, you know, like a mask. Suddenly he's got the axe and he's going after the boat they rowed over on. Back then they still used wood canoes sometimes, and pretty soon he's hacked it all into kindling, *chop-chop-chop*. The others, they're all screaming at him, but he's still got that slack expression on his face, like he's listening to something else, like he's not even there at all. Then when he's finished with the boat, he goes after the other kids. The first one he gets easily—he gets her in the leg first so she can't run, then he splits her skull while she's crawling away from him, *chop-chop-chop*. But the other one makes the killer chase after him. And this kid's a real track star, so he thinks he's safe, only now it's dark and it's such a small island...nowhere really to run. So he does the next best thing. He tries to swim for it..."

"But that doesn't work," Shanna guessed. Hyde only stared up at the dark sky.

"The waves pushed him back," Cameron admitted. "He washed up right at the killer's feet—and that was all she wrote. *Chop-chop-chop*."

Hyde scoffed, but it came out forced, only a puff of air. "Let me guess..." he said. "They never found the bodies. They say the Cabot Island Chopper's *still on this island*, dragging a bloody axe in one hand and a conch in the other, and if you listen *real still* on a quiet night..."

"That's not it," Cameron interrupted. "They found the bodies, all of them. And they found the killer too, crying his eyes out on this beach. He didn't know what had happened to his friends. They found him holding the axe, but he begged innocent anyway. They never found out why he did it. It got him the chair—they still did that back then. They said he wasn't crazy, not in the way that mattered. So he fried. He never confessed. And they never found a conch."

"And that's it?" Shanna's eyes flashed almost angrily. "That's all of it?"

"What more could there be?" he replied miserably. "All right— here's more. My Uncle Jonah never got over it. Sometimes he thinks he should have been there. That he should have stopped it or gotten killed trying. He thinks he would have deserved it. That was all of his friends, you know. Do you get it? All the friends he had."

The last phrase came out of his mouth with too much heat on it; he wanted to clap his hands over his lips, but instead he just drank from the Chairman's Reserve, punishing himself with the bitter burn of the rum. Both of the others stared at him, Hyde with a dull drunken face and Shanna again with that unfathomable nameless expression. For a moment, no one spoke.

Then Hyde let out a belch and stood up suddenly all wobbly. "Well shit, Marine Bio." He seemed impressed enough by this that he said it again. "Well—shit."

"Where are you going?" Cameron asked.

The other boy swiped sand off his hindquarters. "Smoke's getting in my eyes," he rumbled. "Gonna...gonna walk down the beach a bit, before I hit the sack."

He glanced down, held out a hand to Shanna, an invitation. This would be it, the moment that always came. They'd take the picnic blanket and wander off into the darkness. Cameron would wait up for them, but they wouldn't come back, and he'd put the fire out himself and crawl into his tent. In the morning, there they'd be, standing too close together, some secret kind of electricity crackling in the air between them.

Shanna took the other boy's hand, squeezed it—but didn't let him haul her to her feet. "You go on," she said. "Take a flashlight with you. It's gonna get real dark out here."

Cameron thought he saw Hyde's face cloud over. A flash of frustration, then it was gone. He peeled off his shirt, the fire blasting red against his bare chest. "I'll be back soon," he said. "Don't drink all the booze."

He lumbered off, moving unsteadily, flexing and un-flexing his fists beside his hips. The shoreline took a bend. Pretty soon the beam of the flashlight was a line of white on the horizon, and darkness was dropping down all over from the sky.

Shanna's voice startled Cameron out of a haze:

"How'd your Uncle Jonah know all that stuff?"

"What's that?" He looked past the fire at her; she was peering sharply at him, her eyes shiny and dark. She pulled an impatient face and said:

"About how the killer's face looked, and that stuff about the seashell."

"I guess I don't know."

Her expression softened some. "I thought you were fooling for sure." She shifted her bottom in the sand, stretching back to work a kink in her neck. "But some of that was true...wasn't it? At least some part of it."

Cameron's hands knotted in his lap. "There wasn't a conch. Jonah made that part up."

"But the rest...?" Cameron only nodded, not looking at her. "My God...and you still came here as a kid? Your parents brought you here?"

"They didn't see the harm. Our family owns the island, in a roundabout way. They didn't think it would damage me. Guess they learned their lesson. They got pretty sore at Uncle Jonah when they found out he'd told me that story."

"You brought *me* here." Another nod: she waved her hand, prodding him on. "Why?"

"Because..." The bracelet burned in his pocket. "Because I wanted to spend some time with you. Before everything changes. You're transferring, and we're all gonna be seniors before you know it, and after that it's the world. Jobs, wives, lives. All of it. I don't know. It felt like something I needed to do."

She turned away—almost shyly, Cameron thought.

"I still haven't made up my mind about that."

"You're going," he said. "It's a great opportunity. And all that money..."

"All the same." She looked up at the dark sky for a long moment. There weren't stars yet, but the heavens were dark, not black but the darkest blue you ever saw.

"You want to swim?" she asked suddenly. "I think I want to swim."

She was standing up, the firelight glowing under her—she stripped off the Misfits t-shirt, wet from spilled beer. It was hard to look away from what was underneath, but Cameron did anyway, like she was the sun. There was a tattoo across her stomach, one he hadn't seen before. It looked like a snake, or a chain, or a rope. It was too dark to tell, even with the fire there.

"It's gonna be cold," he said numbly. It wasn't cold he was feeling then.

Shanna had the shirt thrown over one shoulder, looking down at him. "You're full of booze—you won't feel it." When he didn't move, she shrugged, her face a mask, lit from below. "Whatever, but if something in the water eats me, you've got to tell my folks."

She turned, prancing toward the surf. Cameron was standing up, pulling off his own shirt, already bracing for the cold. He wasn't wearing a swimsuit, just a pair of jersey shorts, and he tied them tight around his waist before kicking his shoes off and peeling off his socks.

Shanna plunged forward, kicking up spray as the tail of a wave struck her. "Shit—cold!" Her voice shivered, but there was a smile in it. "Come on! Don't make me do this all on my own." He stumbled after her, moving in a sort of fugue. The sun was beneath the horizon now; there was only a wonderful gold stripe across Cabot Town in the distance.

He reached the water's edge—the cold struck through him like an arrow and left him gasping. He felt his breath catch like a hook in his chest, and for a moment he thought his heart had stopped beating altogether. He heard Shanna's splashing a dozen feet or so away, then the noise cut out. She was swimming now instead of wading, almost completely submerged. In the water she seemed to transform, becoming some aquatic creature, a selkie with the skin of a girl instead of a seal. He forced himself forward, after her. Behind them, the fire continued to blaze. He had a sudden thought to put it out, but again, it was Shanna's voice pulling him back.

"Oy—Cam! Over here!"

He looked around for her, but the glare coming off the water was hypnotizing. She wasn't there, and suddenly something wrapped strong tendrils around his leg. He yelped and kicked...it was strong, it wasn't letting go, it was pulling him down, down under the cold water...

"Gotcha, you big pussy." Shanna rose up in front of him, shaking out her hair, too cold to laugh. In the dark she seemed even more naked than she had in her bikini. The dark stripped everything away, leaving only vagueness, the dim outline of a sensuous form.

"Boo yourself," he said. "You wanted to swim. Here we are—freezing our tits off."

"Speak for your own tits. I feel fantastic." She flopped backward, making a game effort to float. "Fucking hell!" she shrieked. "Something touched my leg!"

"That's *my* leg," Cameron said. "You big pussy."

She stood up again, and this time she did laugh, her voice chilly. She wrapped her arms around herself, slapping her body in an X shape.

"What the hell are we doing out here?" she said.

"This was your idea, don't look at me."

"That's not what I meant," Shanna grouched. But she left off, and when she spoke again she'd already changed the subject in her head. "I didn't mean to shit on your story," she said. "Even if it wasn't... I don't know. I don't know why I acted like that."

"You didn't..." he started to say, then couldn't finish. Instead he said: "Do you remember what we did the last night of summer before our senior year, back in high school?"

"Uh-huh. You took your sweet time coming outside. I thought I was gonna pass out on the porch. God, it must have been a hundred degrees. I was sweating like a hog."

"You got your older sister to buy you cigarettes. You wanted me to try one with you."

Shanna shook her head, droplets cascading down from her bangs. "Nuh-uh. I lied about that. I bought them myself, from the gas station Mitch Williams used to work at."

"You're lying." She shook her head again. "You were seventeen. How'd you fudge it?"

"I flashed him," came the reply, without fanfare. She seemed to be studying his face, looking for something there, for some color only she could see. She was facing out of the fading sun, her own features totally engulfed by shadow now.

"Is that right?" he said.

"No—you asshole, you *believed* that?" She slapped the water, like she had with the dolphins. "But I did buy them. He just didn't card me. I wish he had... Now I can't quit them. I've wanted a smoke the whole time we've been on this stupid rock."

Now came Cameron's turn to laugh. "I'm the asshole? You tried to cram one in my mouth that night. You almost burned me, in fact you *did* burn me! A little, on my neck."

"You're right, I did." Again there was a funny note in her voice. Her face said she was teasing again, like she'd always teased him. But there was something sour in the words. "God, I was so mad at myself. I'd thought... I mean, I pictured..."

"What?"

"It's nothing." She turned away slightly, in profile to him. Then she said:

"I really thought you were going to kiss me that night."

The cold water had sobered him up; now there seemed to be no cold at all. No water, no beach, no sky. Again that peculiar thrill shivered across his skin, and his chest felt tight as though he had been holding his breath.

"I don't understand." It was all he could say.

She pressed a hand to her face, covering one eye. He imagined her grinning shyly, even if he couldn't see the grin. "I don't know," she said. "You had this look on your face. You looked, I don't know, brave...like you'd gotten ginned up to *do* something. I'd never seen you look like that. It was like a moment in a movie. And I thought... Well, never mind what I thought. You didn't. And we had a nice time all the same. But it would have been a nice memory. And it's like you said. Now everything's going to change..."

She broke off again, twisting away from him. There were a hundred things he wanted to say to her, but they ran together in his head, his mouth. Her voice had been so hollowed at the end, empty and scraping, with an edge like jagged glass. He had nothing to say that would match that. Instead, he reached out and grabbed hold of her hand—and slipped the bracelet onto her wrist. For a moment she only stared at it. The beads glistened in the last dregs of sunlight. Shanna's breathing was loud, in the middle of all that silence.

"What does it say?" she said in a shivering voice. "I can't see."

"Just your name. Across the beads."

"You made this for me? Like, you *made* this?"

He nodded, wishing he could see her face. "This...could be a nice memory, I guess."

"Fuck, that's..." She held the bracelet close to her face, twisting it on her wrist. He could see her hand quiver slightly. She made a hissing noise between her lips, like she was laughing. Then she turned to face him fully. "I mean..." she said. "I mean..."

She leaned toward him across the water, and he suddenly thought of how she had leaned out of the canoe, after the dolphins. He thought for an instant she might kiss *him*—instead, she plunged forward and threw her arms around his neck, nearly knocking them both into the water. Cameron had to swing them around just to keep balance. Her grip was so tight, and she was shaking against him. She hadn't been laughing. It wasn't until he heard the first gasp that he realized this. It was a terrible noise, coming in chokes and stifled sobs. A painful, wretched sound...

Not knowing what else to do, he put his arms around her. She shuddered, and when she pressed herself against him it was not how she'd snuggled against Hyde in the boat or by the bonfire. It was like hunger, or terror. He let her cry into him. He didn't know what to feel, and so he felt nothing at all. A numbness crept over him that wasn't from the water. He didn't understand. Here again was the signal, the language he didn't speak. Now it was a comfort. He whispered something in her ear, but he'd never remember exactly what he'd told her.

There, just over Shanna's shoulder, a dark form loped and splashed. It was coming toward them. Hyde was coming through the water to meet them.

He could have been anybody in the darkness. He pushed easily through the surf, each muscular movement stiff and powerful. He didn't call out or raise his hand in greeting—he only waded forward, deeper and deeper, not even turning sideways to butt through waves. His hands were low at his sides and his chin was ducked against his chest. Cameron was not sure even that his friend was looking at them or even knew they were there. Cameron let Shanna go, feeling suddenly awkward. She sniffled, wiped her nose, turning to see what he was looking at.

"Jesus..." she said, scrubbing at her eyes. "You *scared* me. Now what's..."

"*Chop-chop-chop*," the other boy said in a voice as smooth and dull as lead.

Cameron didn't see the hatchet until it was almost too late.

Time seemed to crawl, then shuddered forward, like a record skip. Hyde's arm raised up, coming down in a quick and terrible arc... Cameron barely managed to raise his hands above his face. The other boy was stronger, and Cameron couldn't deflect the blow entirely. He felt the blade glance off his forearm—then he was clubbed away by the force of the impact and stumbled back into the water with a shout. He pitched backward, plunging under the dark water. There was no pain, only a sudden ache in his arm and the huge terrible shock of the cold. He thrashed to his feet, coughing violently, shaking, wiping salt water out of his eyes.

The other boy had Shanna by a massive fistful of hair. She was low in the water, seeming to dangle—like the head was all there was. But her lips moved, and a shaky voice came out.

"Cam..." she croaked out. "You can't..."

The hatchet swung down, into her neck. Shanna stopped talking.

Hyde turned a dark slack face toward him, and Cameron found his scream.

Then he was plunging headlong through black water toward the shore. The embers of the bonfire swam, seemed to careen back and forth across the horizon. Twice he stumbled, crashing into cold wet darkness, the waves turning him end over end, but instinct kept him moving forward, not even bothering to look back. The image of Shanna's dead dark mouth falling open swam up in front of his eyes, stark against the night.

Her eyes hadn't closed, a voice screamed inside him. *You didn't know she was dead. You didn't know for sure, but you ran, coward coward coward...*

Then the shore rose up under him, and he fell on his knees, cold water rushing out between his legs as a wave pulled back. He pulled himself hand over hand up the beach, sand gritting down into his bleeding arm—his arm! Good God, there was blood pouring out of it, dark and watery, flowing down his wrist and between his fingers. Still there was no pain somehow, but he let out a yelp anyway, and kept crawling. Finally he got to his feet, stumbling a few more steps toward the fire before he looked back at the water. He pressed his other hand to his gashed forearm. His eyes scanned the water, the shoreline, looking for movement. But all he saw was the distant lights of Cabot Town on the mainland, winking on and off.

No Shanna. And no Hyde, swinging a hatchet.

Then—a cough, off to his right. "H-h-h-h..." A huge dark figure rose up from the surf, shaking off a spray of water. Hyde bent at the waist, with his hands on his knees, hacking water out of his lungs. And Cameron was running again, scrabbling up the beach and into the trees.

Darkness swallowed him down. Branches whipped his face, clawed at his bare skin. His clothes, his shoes and socks, all down on the beach by the fire. Now there was no water to hide the sound of the other boy crashing through behind him. But when Cameron listened, all he heard was the crunch of his own footfalls and his own huffing breaths.

The ground under his feet was sandy and bristled with burrs and stiff prickly grasses. He had to clamp a hand over his mouth when something stabbed into his foot, biting his fingers to keep from screaming, tasting his own blood. He stumbled forward, finally tumbling down into a hollow carved out by the roots of a long-dead tree. He looked up, half-expecting to see the towering shape of Hyde—of the killer, the killer who'd slipped on Hyde's face and form—staring down at him.

But he was alone. So he hunkered down, sucking on his bloody fingers, keeping pressure on his wounded aching arm. He listened...

"You let him kill me, Cameron."

It wasn't real. But he squeezed his eyes shut, and there in that darkness he saw it again, Shanna's mouth falling open slack, blood pouring out. Her ruined lips moved grotesquely, blood-slick and jerky in their movements, like a dead thing should move.

"You wanted me. Is that supposed to be special? Everybody wanted me."

The jaws sagged open, wider and wider.

"I guess you didn't want me bad enough."

"Shut up," he cried into his hands. "Shut up, shut up, *shut up...*"

"Hyde loved me. He showed me how much he loved me."

"Why can't you just leave me alone?"

The yawning mouth chuckled, not moving at all now.

"You were always alone. We're moving on...and now, you're going to move on too."

Cameron opened his eyes, straining his ears. There was movement in the forest. Something crunched not twenty feet from where he lay, moving steadily past him. Something grunted and huffed—it was not Hyde, it could not be Hyde. Humans did not make noises like that. This was a low sound, without consciousness. An animal sound. It was moving away from him, up the slope, toward the peak of the island.

"Chop-chop-chop..." muttered a voice through the scrub. *"Chop-chop-chop..."*

The killer moved on, and Cameron could not hear its footsteps any longer. Shanna did not speak again. And now he was running, running, running toward the beach.

He reached the last steep incline, nearly blind now. The night was a curtain of shadow, draped across everything. He turned his ankle on a rock and tumbled down through the sand...when he yelped, his mouth filled up with grit and he spat it out, brushing his tongue along his bare arm. On the beach, there was no one. The thin stripe of sand wiggled away to his left, his right. All over, everything was bathed in moonlight. The fire was embers now; he picked his way toward it, nursing his ankle. His foot struck something half-buried: Hyde's flashlight, the battery cap unscrewed. He groped in the sand for the loose battery, found it, slid it home.

The light blazed to life; he quickly hooded it with his hand, only letting a little bit of glow through. In the beam, the sand under his feet was bone white, barren, like the surface of the moon. He swept the light along the treeline in a quick flash. Nothing stirred.

Then the edge of the water—Cameron's breath caught like Velcro in his lungs. It was Shanna, lying half in the surf, face up. She'd washed ashore, almost at his feet. He limped toward her, praying, hoping against all hope...but when he was closer he felt all his strength drain away. Her eyes were open, looking up at the dark of the heavens. Her hair was matted on one side of her face from all the blood, but this was already drying in the restless ocean breeze. He saw, in brief flashes, her wounds: a chunk carved out of her shoulder, her crushed and bleeding throat, a cake-slice of skull. There was red and gray leaking from this last wound, flowing out onto the sand, where the tide lapped it up and carried it off.

Cameron didn't feel the vomit coming. He simply turned his head and it appeared, coming out of him. Then he wiped his mouth and he wept—silently, so Hyde wouldn't hear and come running with the hatchet, *chop-chop-chop*...

He'd fallen on his knees a few feet from the corpse, and when he picked himself up again, he let the light play along the beach-scrub where they'd hidden the canoe, moving it higher and higher up the hill. Still nothing stirred there. No Hyde, loping blindly through the dark. No scuttling crabs, no wheeling gulls or nightbirds. The surf crashed and crashed at his back. He turned the light there again, moving down the beach. A ways off: something bulged under a receding wave, something smooth and glistening and pink. Cameron retched, visions of severed things dancing in his head, feet or breasts or hunks of buttock.

But it wasn't flesh. It was a conch, lying in the surf, just as Shanna had. A conch as big as two fists put together, with spines running along the edge and around the spire.

Hyde holding the conch, holding it to his ear, his face going slack like...

It was in his hands now. Cameron was standing with one foot in the water, turning the smooth shell over and over. Was it the same as the picture his Uncle Jonah had showed him? Did it twist the same way? Were there three spines along that outer lip, or four? He whirled, jumping at shadows, flicking the flashlight beam out into the darkness. That had been a footstep, hadn't it? Crunching the sand under a heavy heel?

Had that been a breath caught short?

No...he was alone on the beach. The dark seemed infinite, cut by the flashlight's beam.

Slowly he put the conch up close to his ear. The night closed in, crushing in from everywhere. He didn't think about Shanna, or Hyde lurking somewhere in the dark. Slowly it all drained out of him: the fear, the cold, the pain in his arm. The world spun crazily, and blood flowed out of his forearm, falling on his knees and the sand beneath. No—not from his arm...

From the blade tooth of the hatchet, dangling head-down in his other hand...

He only stared at it a moment. The flashlight flickered once, then winked off. All dark now. No light but the stars and the moon and the eyes of Cabot Town over the water; no sound but the ocean and the wind. No motion but the gentle waves. The world had moved on.

Cameron kept his ear pressed to the open lips of the conch. The hatchet, still slick with blood, lay at his feet; perhaps it had been there before. Perhaps it had always been. He listened for a long time, and slowly he began to weep again, louder and louder. He didn't hear Hyde slinking behind the curtain of the darkness, or Shanna's wet mocking voice.

What he heard was the ocean—but whether it came from the rushing surf, or from within the shell, or from inside himself somewhere, nobody could answer.

The following email chain and attached documents were recovered from the PC of Joel Mackie, feature writer for the online dark fiction publication RISING DARK REVIEW. All audio components are transcribed; all visual elements are described in text. These records were released online 10 December 2019 and are believed genuine.

Together, they form the narrative known to online theorists everywhere as:

The Panic

SENT: Monday, 10/11/2004
TO: dclarkes@risingdarkmag.com
FROM: jmackie@risingdarkmag.com
RE: Spontaneous Mass Drowning Event – Sanibel Island, FL

Dahlia,

Sorry for the radio silence—I've been whupped by that stomach bug that's been going around. But I wanted to let you know I'm just about done compiling the docs my contact on Sanibel's been forwarding. There's loads here but if you've got time over the long weekend, let's look these over together. I dunno if there's a story here or if Bembe's pulling another stunt. But just the same, you should see what he's sent my way.

Here's truth: Maybe I'm still queasy from that stomach thing, but when I got all this together I felt...unsettled, somehow. Part of me hopes this is all some big prank on us. But another part—the sick [redacted] part, I guess—wants it to be true.

That nuts or what? Guess it's why I work here.

I've attached all the relevant stuff. There's multiple different docs—so let me know if anything doesn't come through. Our mail system's been jacked up recently...think it's a memory issue maybe? Or storage problems? I hope it hasn't affected submissions. Let's talk soon. Friday evening maybe?

Joel Mackie

Feature Writer, *Rising Dark Review*

Ø

ATTACHED: sanibelseafoam1.pdf

Sanibel Island "Sea Foam" Newsletter – 8/6/2004

Hey Beach Bums...

We interrupt our regularly scheduled reporting on Summer Fun-in-the-Sun to bring you this bulletin: Island PD's search for the beachgoers who vanished during the July 31 anomaly is yet ongoing. Investigators are asking the public for any information they might have as to the missing individuals' whereabouts. Eyewitnesses to the event are encouraged to report to SIPD headquarters or call the tip line provided at the bottom of the page. Counseling will be available for respondents under 18.

Stay fresh, small fry...

Flat-Fish Frankie

ATTACHED: sanibelvacation2014-34.jpg

The attached file is a scan of a photograph believed taken during the July 31 event. The image depicts a beach scene, with the photographer facing the ocean. Objects in the foreground appear out of focus; water damage has obscured figures in the bottom-right corner of frame. Several dozen adult figures face away from the camera, also looking toward the water. They appear in motion, moving toward the surf. Some are half-in, half-out of the ocean; more are already mostly or entirely submerged. In the distance a smaller shape appears: likely a fishing vessel or other craft. A young boy's face appears in profile in the foreground, but water damage and poor focus obscure his expression.

The photographer's identity is unknown.

ATTACHED: sanibellifeguardreport.docx

31 July 2004 – 2:51 PM – Incident Report (Yelt): Saw victim [name redacted] enter water approx. 2 PM day of reporting. Had observed victim with family before, appeared a strong swimmer. Resumed standard scanning. After 2 scan cycles, did not notice victim in water. Began deliberated scanning—still did not locate victim. Stood and delivered double blast on whistle, at which point trainee Lee Kim took over chair.

Entered water where victim had entered: found him floating head-up only a few dozen feet from shore. Surf conditions were smooth; victim was easy to spot and reach. Performed standard single-guard rescue. Victim had open eyes but appeared unconscious, and resumed breathing when his head cleared water. Reached shore—Lee Kim and full-time guard Jared Osman assisted with backboard extraction.

Victim [redacted] regained consciousness soon after landfall and became disoriented, trying multiple times to reenter the water. Restraining victim took 3 guards, me included. Jared Osman sustained a cut above left eye. Responding guard suffered broken ribs on right side. Lee Kim was uninjured but shaken. Victim's current condition unknown. By time of rescue (approx. 2:15) crowds had gathered by shore: victim left lifeguard care and disappeared.

2 August 2004 – 4:14 PM – Addendum (Yelt): *None* of us saw the others at first. Then there were too many to miss. I had busted ribs—Jared was still bleeding out of his face. What did you want us to do? It was too late for most of them anyway. We helped who we could help. We did our [redacted] jobs.

Signed: Helen Yelt, SG (senior guard)
Cosigned: Jared Osman, HG (head guard) and Lee Kim (trainee)

ATTACHED: sleeplesshour-season4-ep13-rip.mp3

Dahlia—here's a fragment of that "true horror" podcast I've been yakking about, The Sleepless Hour. *I think they did a series about the July 31 event, but everything they did on the drownings got nixed off the host platform. Bembe was able to find somebody who'd uploaded part of this episode: it's pretty corrupted, but I've cleaned it up some. You can't really hear the guy asking questions, but the other guy's audible enough.*

[speaker 1] Yanni Thomasin...19.

[speaker 1] All my life, near enough.

[speaker 1] I don't take my phone out on my kayak. But I guess around 2. Me and Hungry Mike had eaten lunch. [...] Oh...21. He'd just had a birthday.

[speaker 1] Screaming, coming from the beach. Thought somebody'd seen a shark.

[speaker 1] Nothing at first. Then...it was like a footrace starting in slow-motion. They all started coming toward me into the water.

[speaker 1] Hundreds. Hell, maybe a thousand. [...] From both directions on the beach.

[speaker 1] All adults. It was the kids screaming. *Their* kids, I guess.

[speaker 1] Not to start. Then they didn't come back up. I got real nervous after that.

[speaker 1] When I heard the splash.

[speaker 1] His kayak was just kind of rocking there. I don't know what happened to the paddle.
They're supposed to float. I guess he took it with him.

[speaker 1] The water was pretty clear...but no. I looked for almost an hour. Then I had to get on shore quick. I left his kayak in the water. I didn't wanna touch it.

[speaker 1] His mom and his little brother. They weren't on the beach. Lucky them.

[speaker 1] If you're talking about that fishing boat, no. I was looking toward shore most of the time. If it was there, I was between it and the beach.

[speaker 1] Local police, then later some other government goons. They asked a lot of the same questions, and I started getting pretty sore about it.

[speaker 1] Not to talk about this to *anybody*.

ATTACHED: WGSITV-2014clip1.mov

The attached video file is archival footage from WGSI, a now-defunct local news station on Sanibel Island. The footage was ripped from the station's YouTube page, also inactive; the clip has long been taken down from the channel itself, and no reuploads appear on other sites. The clip depicts a Sanibel native, identified as "Trish," giving an interview sometime after the July 31 event. Police lights flash in the background. The screams of gulls permeate the audio.

[trish molloy] No—this was before everybody went nuts. Maybe 10 minutes before.

[trish molloy] About a quarter mile offshore, maybe?

[trish molloy] I dunno. I guess something just didn't look right about it.

[trish molloy] No gulls. You see fishing boats out all the time, and there's always a whole mess of seagulls hanging around them. But this one didn't have one.

[trish molloy] Kinda fake-looking. Like a toy or a prop. You know in *Jaws*, how the shark they used only had half a body so they could operate it from the other side? It looked like that, like there was only half a boat there. The half we were supposed to see.

[trish molloy] Well, it *had* to be a boat. There were people on it, yeah? I told that other crew already. Don't you all talk to each other?

[trish molloy] 3 or 4 guys, all in these yellow slicker coats. Only, the arms of the coats were too long...maybe the arms themselves were too long? They dragged on the deck of the fishing boat, and they kind of...flapped around. It wasn't exactly walking, what they were doing, and it wasn't exactly jumping.

[trish molloy] Mostly their faces. They were smooth all over. Egg-smooth. Or like a toilet bowl. White like that too. Not pale but *white*. Like paper.

[trish molloy] It was cruising along the beach, north to south. It wasn't moving crazy fast, but it was definitely moving.

[trish molloy] Well—all that screaming started. I lost track of it for a moment or two. Somebody kicked over my chair on their way to the water.

[trish molloy] Maybe ten minutes?

[trish molloy] I guess there was some haze or fog out there because I couldn't find it again through the binoculars. It just kind of vanished.

[trish molloy] Not for another 8 months.

Ø

SENT: Thursday, 10/14/2004
TO: dclarkes@risingdarkmag.com
FROM: jmackie@risingdarkmag.com
RE: Spontaneous Mass Drowning Event – Sanibel Island, FL

Dahlia,

Why didn't you say the rest of the docs didn't upload? We're lucky I was going through my Sent folder and spotted it. We've got to get that new IT guy to take a look at our server's memory issues if this keeps on happening.

Anyhoo: I talked to Bembe on the phone right after I fired off that last email and he said he'd got new stuff for me. He sounded a little shaky, but I don't know if that was because he had bad reception or something. But this new batch of docs... Dahlia, this is good stuff. I still don't know if he's pulling something, but if these are fakes then they're great fakes. I'm half-convinced we should just post scans on the site and let the fans sort it out themselves.

Let me know when's a good time to call. I wish I could see your face when you read it all the first time, but I'll settle for the play-by-play.

TTFN,

Joel

PS: Bembe says he wants to talk to you—in person. I dunno if it's a good idea, but I'll leave it up to you. He *did* sound shaky on that phone call.

Ø

ATTACHED: sanibelclarion-writein.pdf

Sanibel Island *Clarion* – We Want to Hear from You! – 8/10/2014

This for all you Real Nice Folks who've been calling and showing up at the house all hours of the night. Yes, I've seen the pictures. Yes, I *used* to own a fishing boat that looked a *little* like that one. But I'll tell you: There's no way that boat you think you saw is mine, coz the Panic hit a reef near 2 years ago. It's at the bottom of the ocean and it ought to stay there for all I care. I just want you Real Nice Folks to quit hassling me about old news. I served my country 2 times. I got a finger blown off in Korea. I'm 70 and I'm too old to deal with your [redacted]. Leave me and my wife alone. – *Burton Groose, Sanibel Island resident*

ATTACHED: voicemail.mp3

[breathing]

Daddy? [...] Come on, pick up, pick up... [...] Okay. Okay. Daddy, you said if I ever got really scared somewhere you would come get me. And you wouldn't ask me any questions about it? Something...happened on the beach today. And I know this is

Mommy's cell phone but Mommy's not... I mean, she can't... [...] Everybody just went into the water all together. There was a Bad Boat out in the water, and then everybody went in the water. Mommy was...

[breathing, soft crying]

Mommy was holding Fletcher when she went in. And he was struggling and crying but she wouldn't let go and I couldn't stop her. I know you said I'm a big strong boy now, but I couldn't stop her from going in. She was dragging me along. And once she got to the water... [...] Daddy, please don't be mad. But I let go. I couldn't...I couldn't go into that water with them. She wouldn't even talk to me. She wouldn't even *look* at me. She just kept walking, and Fletcher, he kept wiggling and yelling and...

[breathing]

He stopped crying once his head went underwater. Then I couldn't see them anymore. Mommy was one of the last ones to go in. [...] There's no grown-ups on the beach anymore. Maybe there's no grownups anywhere.

[breathing, crying]

Please come pick me up. I don't wanna be here anymore. But don't come out on the beach. I can come out on the street, there's a walkway here. Number 11. Don't come looking for me. They took all the grownups on the beach, and they'll take you too. *The Bad Boat will take you too.*

[breathing]

I love you, Daddy. And I'm real sorry.

ATTACHED: sanibelseafoam2.pdf

Sanibel "Sea Foam" Newsletter – 8/13/2004
Hey Beach Bums...

Summer fun-in-the-sun gives way to gloomy clouds today. Area organizers have announced that public memorial services for victims of the July 31 drowning event will be held on Lightfoot Pier over the coming weekend. Further details, along with a full list of the missing/deceased, can be found on the website linked to this QR code.

Stay crispy, small fry...

Flat-Fish Frankie

ATTACHED: satelliteimage1

The attached image files comprise satellite images captured off Bowman's Beach on 31 July 2014, apparently before or during the event itself. All 3 images depict a fishing vessel from 3 different angles as captured by the flight of the satellite: one from directly overhead, one from the front of the craft, and one from a side angle. Each image is grainy and distorted from enlarging a low-resolution image, and parts of the photos appear incomplete, as though there are whole clusters of pixels missing.

The side view image reveals symbols painted along the hull: at first examination they appear to spell the name *Panic*, but closer inspection reveals that they don't comprise recognizable human letters. In each image, figures wearing yellow coats appear on the deck of the craft in bizarre poses. The number of these figures changes from image to image: 3 in the first, 2 in the second, and 5 in the third. Image distortion gives these figures disproportionately long arms, and their faces are uniformly round and pale. No matter how many appear in each image, one is always facing the camera.

Ø

SENT: Sunday, 10/17/2004
TO: dclarkes@risingdarkmag.com
FROM: jmackie@risingdarkmag.com
RE: Spontaneous Mass Drowning Event – Sanibel Island, FL
Dahlia,

Is everything okay? I'm worried I haven't heard back after 2 emails. It's not like you to go dark...but I'm sure you've got your reasons. Just shoot me a message when you've gone through all this stuff, including what I'm forwarding you here.

Honestly: If anything's worrying me now, it's Bembe. I can't get him on the phone, and his last emails haven't had any text in them. They're just doc-dumps. It's still interesting stuff, but I'm baffled why he's shut me out. I tried baiting him, saying you'd talk to him if he called me back, but he didn't bite at that. His social media's gone dark too, and all his profile pictures are that stock silhouette now.

I dunno how to move forward here. This is all new territory for me.

Ping me when you're done with the materials—I'll let you make the call.

Joel

Ø

ATTACHED: journal-SIPD.pdf (scan 2)

Journal Entry 29 August 2014 – Detective Redd Yelt

Keep tumbling it in my head, over and over. Case won't click shut, won't fly open. Won't quit. Getting sick, looking at missing faces on posters. Whole thing got wrote down "Missing Persons"— but that ain't what this is, right? 450 souls don't go "missing" They *vanish*. They get disappeared, like they used to do in Russia. Maybe still do.

Fact: Approx. 450 adult beachgoers go missing 31 July.
Fact: Eyewitnesses say victims walked into ocean on their own.
Fact: Same eyewitnesses all kids or young people...
Fact: Victims of 31 July all aged 21 up, male and female.

Fact: Affected area—1 mile stretch of Bowman's Beach, markers 11 and 12. No victims reported save who was on the sand or in the water.

Fact: 31 July coincides with arrival of fishing vessel *Panic*—owner, Burton Groose.

Fact: Groose disputes previous finding but remains person of interest.

Fact: Vid surveillance from hotel Armistice shows 31 July event in progress. Victims enter water as vessel passes by their position on shore. Result—"wave" of bodies entering ocean together.

Fact: Coast Guard divers report no bodies recovered from affected site.

Conclusion: THE WORLD'S LOSING ITS [redacted] MIND.

Guess I could be more logical than that. But it gnaws at me still. Too many loose wires. That damned boat for instance—girl on the news said crazy things, but she was higher than giraffe teeth. Her word's no good for evidence. But how she described the men, the *things*, on the deck...even if it was some goofy hallucination, I can't get the picture out of my head. Long creatures in yellow coats, jumping and flapping...

There's the thing: I've talked to other officers on the case, and they can't get it out of their brains either. Like it's invaded us. Like it burned into our skulls. Clancy Hunt's not even in Missing Persons...he only heard the scuttlebutt through channels. He told me he went out once and stood on that beach and just kind of stared at the water. For four hours. Christ, he didn't even stop to pee. It had hold of him that bad.

Worst thing is, I can picture me doing that. I *want* to do it.

And there's more, isn't there? Helen lifeguards on that beach. She's got some vacation they're giving her now, but next summer for sure she'll have to go back unless she finds some other job. She's scared I think, but she's tough. My money says she'll stick in place. She takes after Maureen like that. She'll be out there, getting tanned as toast and having all the boys holler down the beach at her.

But her birthday's 11 June. Most of that summer—she'll be 21.

ATTACHED: sanibelseafoam3.pdf

Sanibel Island "Sea Foam" Newsletter – 9/01/2004

Hey Beach Bums...

This may be the last you hear from good old Pan-Fried, Leather-Lipped Flat-Fish Frankie. Those notorious do-gooders—you know 'em, the Alphabet People—stormed into Uncle Frankie's news shack and *took it all.* File cabinet, items pinned on walls, even my Little Black Book. They even took my laptop—which is why this missive's getting click-clacked by typewriter.

Here's worse, if you've got the stomach: I'm not the only Beach Bum these Dudley Do-Wrongs rolled. Your favorite Flat-Fish keeps ear to ground, and I've heard stories all over about folks getting roughed, hassled, and generally put ill-at-ease over this July 31 dust-up. It's true-blue police-state tom-foolery, and bet your bottom dollar Frankie's not gonna take it...no sirree Bob!

But for now: strategic retreat's in order, a quick-trick getaway from Sunny Sanibel's shores to dream up some new scheme to get word out to you loyal Bottom-Feeders. Lucky for me, there's always a beach somewhere. You float up my way, stop in for a cool-breeze brew, and as always:

Stay low, small fry...

Flat-Fish Frankie

ATTACHED: badboat-sightings.pdf

Attached file contains a scan of a hand-drawn map of Sanibel Island and surrounding landmasses, with several additions made in red pen along with handwritten labels and notes. First of these is a red line denoting a 1-mile stretch of Bowman's Beach, along with a letter X drawn offshore. Further out, more Xs appear with a line connecting them. These points were once labeled with dates, but the scan's resolution isn't high enough for these to be reliably legible.

Notes scrawled in the margins read:

"Never approaches shore."

"Never gets close enough."
"What is it *waiting* for?"
"Goddammit, Goddammit, Goddammit..."
"Are we still safe?"
"What does it WANT??"

A crude drawing appears in the bottom-right corner of the image, depicting a figure in a slicker coat with a hood. The drawing's face is simply a yawning toothless hole.

ATTACHED: headlines.docx.

Wulfert resort opens investigation into vanished seniors – Sanibel *Clarion*, 8/30/2014

Ft. Myers Beach closed, linked to missing joggers case – Sanibel *Clarion*, 9/13/2014

Ybel lighthouse keeper fourth to disappear – Sanibel *Clarion*, 9/21/2014

Ø

SENT: Monday, 10/24/2004
TO: dclarkes@risingdarkmag.com
FROM: jmackie@risingdarkmag.com
RE: Spontaneous Mass Drowning Event – Sanibel Island, FL

Dahlia,

Got hold of Bembe—or I should say, he got hold of me. He sounded bad last night. Freaking out in a major way... I didn't like how he was running his mouth, but I got him calm enough to tell me: he's moving off Sanibel. He wouldn't tell me where. All he'd say was "further inland" and that we shouldn't look him up. He said he'd seen the "bad boat" in his head, it's all he can think about now. That was it for him—when he woke up 20 miles from his apartment, face up on Bowman's Beach. He thinks it's coming back, I mean he really thinks it. He said a lot more crazy stuff like that, but the worst was when I tried to ask him why it was coming back. I could picture his face, looking at me like I was the biggest damn fool on the planet.

"For the rest of us," he said. "It's coming back for the ones it missed before."

That's when I got to putting 2 and 2 together. I've got no idea when Bembe's birthday is, but I bet you it's soon—or it already happened. I bet he's just turned 21.

I'd been feeling funny about all this before, but now I know it: we've gotta run with this story. It could be huge for us, fake or not fake. But there's still more we need, and if Bembe's not gonna send it up our way, I've got no other option, right? I've got some vacay coming up, so it won't be on company time—I'm gonna wager it all on Sunny Sanibel, like our friend Flat-Fish Frankie would call it. I know you're reluctant. I understand your silence now. But you'll understand once I've seen it for myself. You'll understand it all, I know you will. We're so close, Dahlia. It's like I can reach out and touch it. I can almost picture it in my head now.

I don't hit 21 for another 2 weeks. That should buy me enough time.

(I can PICTURE it, Dahlia, so clear so clear)

Joel

Ø

SENT: Monday, 10/24/2004
TO: jmackie@risingdarkmag.com
FROM: dclarkes@risingdarkmag.com
RE: Spontaneous Mass Drowning Event – Sanibel Island, FL

Joel—call me please ASAP!!!

Ø

SENT: Monday, 10/24/2004
TO: dclarkes@risingdarkmag.com

FROM: Mailer-daemon@googlemail.com
RE: Spontaneous Mass Drowning Event – Sanibel Island, FL

Address not found.

Your message wasn't delivered to: jmackie@risingdarkmag.com because the address couldn't be found, or is unable to receive mail.

LEARN MORE NOW?

Some Bad Luck Near Bitter Downs

A strange wind blew out of town, sweeping through the dust; it smelled of killing, and there had been some killing only hours ago. Now the blood had soaked into the thirsty ground and the world lay still. Outside of Bitter Downs, the riders were in retreat.

Two men on horseback came over the low ridge, the sun at their backs. It had been ten miles of hard riding; now the pace of their horses slowed, threading down between the cacti. One of them bent low in the saddle. He was the younger of the two brothers; there was a bullet in his stomach, and it was spilling blood down the front of him, into his lap and onto the saddle. The other man wiped his brow and stared at the sky, then back along the ridgeline, peering at the rocks and the shadows under them. There was a black leather satchel tied to his saddle; it bounced against the horse's flank in easy rhythm.

He called whoa to his horse and dismounted. A distance off, a dry creek bed slithered through the dust. The older brother looked at his companion, who coughed and did not speak.

The older brother said: "This is far enough, I guess we'll make camp."

There was a cloth tied around his neck, which had previously disguised his face. He untied it and wiped his mouth and his cheeks. His younger brother dismounted as well, wincing against the pain of his midsection. He too unwound the cloth from his neck and pressed it against his wound, soaking up some of the blood. He said: "Pass over that whiskey, I'm hurt bad."

"I guess you are."

The older man dug in his saddle bag and fetched the whiskey, bringing it over. The younger brother splashed it on his stomach and hissed through his teeth. Then he put the bottom of the bottle toward the sky and drank. The older brother got the bedrolls down from the horses and walked down into the creek bed with them. The younger man called down the slope after him:

"Never mind making camp now. I want to count that money."

The reply came up: "So go on and count it."

The younger man said: "You're sore with me. Don't be sore, I'm a dying man."

"You're not dying. You're bleeding. Grown men bleed sometimes."

"Don't be sore with me. I didn't mean for it to happen."

The older brother looked up out of the creek bed. He said: "The hell you didn't."

He came up the dusty slope, taking long careful strides. His younger brother was half-splayed against a large stone, out of the sun, with his legs going out different directions. His hat was cockeyed on his head, and the whiskey bottle was still in his hand. There was less in the bottle now, a lot less. His face was red under the shade of the rock. He said:

"I don't see why that boy had to jump up like that anyhow."

The older brother moved back toward the horses, settling the feed bags around their noses. He said: "I guess you spooked him. You were pointing a gun at his paw."

"Well—he shouldn't have jumped up like that."

"He wasn't grown enough to shoot. You throw fry like him back."

"He jumped up. I didn't know if he had a gun."

"He couldn't have lifted a gun, much less fired it."

"I didn't see how big he was. I just saw him jump up. That's his bad luck."

The older brother considered this uneasily. Images passed though his mind, of the fat man in the dark suit standing up from the wagon, his mouth open in a shout; of the scrawny boy falling down through the air toward the dusty ground, his face covered in blood. He remembered shouting himself, then pulling the trigger again and again. For an instant he could smell cordite smoke in the air. Then he was back in himself, staring at his brother. The younger man's face had clouded over, half from pain and half from some other discomfort.

The older brother said: "I guess it didn't help him much. It didn't help his paw any."

The other repeated: "It was just his bad luck."

"I'm starting to think that way."

The younger man handed up the bottle of whiskey. His brother took it, drank. It was good going down and washed the dust out of his throat, but it didn't wash out the other bad feeling. It gnawed in him like a rat gnawing out of a crate. The fat man standing up, reaching for something behind the seat of the wagon, face red with grief and fury...

His brother said: "I bet you counting that money might cool us off."

The older man squinted at the sky again. There was bright light along the ridge where the sun had been, but the heavens in the east were darkening. He pushed his hat forward on his head and turned back toward the horses. He said: "I bet you it could do that."

The satchel was heavy and solid-feeling, like a stuffed critter full-tight with cotton and sawdust. It felt good in the older brother's hands as he unfastened it from the saddle and brought it over to the rock where the younger man lay sprawled. He sat like a redskin, crossing his legs underneath him, and set the satchel in the dust between him and his brother. The younger man leaned forward eagerly, wetting his dry lips with his tongue.

The older brother undid the latch. For a moment, he stared down into the dark leather mouth of the satchel. Then he scooted back very quickly on his bottom, moving like a crab crawling along the shore. Sweat stood out all along his forehead. He said: "Jesus, Mary, and Joseph..."

There was no money inside. It was a man's head, cut off just at the neck.

The younger brother gaped, first at the satchel, then at the other man. No sound came out when his lip flapped up and down. The head was the same color as book paper; the skin was stretched thin across the skull and the eyelids were thin enough to look through, showing colorless eyes under them; the hair was pale and stringy and stiff, long as a woman's hair grows; the lips were pulled back over sharp white teeth fixed in a jaw that was clamped tight. The cut edge, where the neck would meet the shoulders on a body, was smooth as a canoe-bottom. There was no blood anywhere. Through the gauzy eyelids, the head stared at the darkening sky.

The older brother said again: "Jesus, Mary, and Joseph..."

It sounded like fool talk, spoken in that hot lonely place, but there was nothing else he could think of saying. He looked across at his younger brother; he was leaning over the satchel, up on his hands and knees, looking down into it. The older man called out: "You get away from that."

Without looking up, the younger brother called back: "How's that now?"

"I said, you get away from that. Don't go pawing at it."

The younger man retracted his hand, which had snaked toward the opening of the satchel. He looked at his older brother at last; there was a dazed expression on his face, like he was a reflection in smudged glass. He hollered out, a little too loudly: "Where's the money?"

"You half-wit—you snatched the wrong satchel."

"The hell I did."

"Well, does that look like our money?"

"There wasn't but the one satchel in the wagon."

"It looks like a man's head."

"Don't get harsh with me, I know what a man's head looks like."

The younger man's eyes flashed anger; that was good, it sharpened him up some. He heaved up on his feet and kicked at the satchel with the toe of one boot. Somewhere in the glooming sky, a wheeling hawk screamed. The younger man followed the sound with his eyes but did not spot the bird, and pretty soon he gave up looking. At last, he said:

"Hell—I guess that half-wit redskin lied to us."

The older brother had the whiskey at his lips, and he lowered it slowly. He said:

"How do you figure that?"

"Well, isn't that a redskin's head?"

"You can't tell that."

"It is—you look at him and tell me it's not a redskin's head."

The older man didn't move. He just looked at the satchel from where he was. All he said was this: "All right, maybe it's a redskin head. How would our redskin know it was there?"

"Maybe he lost it and thought we'd get it back for him."

"That wasn't so smart of our redskin."

The older brother blew air out of his mouth and said nothing. The younger man put two fingers under the brim of his hat and scratched at his scalp. He went on saying:

"I guess a redskin would say anything to get out of the fix we had him in."

"I guess he would. I might have said anything too."

"Not that it helped him so much."

"I guess it didn't."

The younger man kicked the satchel again with a boot toe. He said: "So who do you think our friend here is, if not a redskin?"

The older brother slugged whiskey and walked forward, peering down again into the leather satchel. The head's eyelids were so thin, they might as well have been open. He could see their pale color, staring upward blindly. He said: "A son of a gun with worse luck than us."

The younger man agreed, sounding a little disappointed: "Bad luck all over."

He knelt and fastened up the satchel with clumsy movements. The whiskey had got hold of him, and he moved like his hands and arms were full of mud. He said: "How do you want to go forward now? Leave it be here, or bury it in the desert?"

"I'll think on it."

"I reckon we bury it. Better than..."

"I said, I'll think on it. You go on and get your bedroll set. You're sitting up first tonight. I don't want some posse creeping down on us while we're sleeping."

His younger brother made a noise under his breath. The older man said: "How's that now?"

"You shouldn't have called me a half-wit."

"Go on and get your bedroll."

"I said, you shouldn't have called me a half-wit. It's not my fault there wasn't any money. That's just bad luck. And the boy was bad luck too."

The older brother had pulled his boots off and put his socks in them, and had slipped halfway into his bedroll in his bare feet. He squinted up the bank of the creek bed. The air was gloomier now, but he could still see his younger brother's face, standing in profile against the sky. The dark twisted up his features; for a moment he was their father, in the grave ten years. He was the fat man in the wagon, spinning away from a bullet. He was the boy bleeding in the dust.

The older man rubbed his face, then lay back. He said: "All right, I shouldn't have said it."

The younger brother didn't speak. He only moved toward the horses. The front of his stomach had dried; the cotton fabric felt brittle and stiff against his skin. The whisky meant it didn't hurt to breathe so much anymore, and now he could walk without wincing. He got his bedroll and laid it out beside his older brother, then climbed back out of the creek bed. The sun was only a thin ribbon up on the ridge, a glow seen through shut eyelids. He got the horses secure and leaned up against a rock, staring up at the ridge they'd come down, and waited for darkness.

Ø

The younger man's eyelids fluttered. For a moment, there was no difference in the light when his eyes were open and when they were closed. Then the world began to sharpen up. There was only a sliver moon; its cracked-tooth smile gave off weak light, like watery milk. The young man could see the ridge looming above him. There behind him were the horses, and to his front was the other jutting rock he had rested beneath before. In front of this was the dim form of the satchel, now shut tight. A little cool wind had kicked up, coming out of the west, from town.

The young man did not shudder. He had not dreamed. He had not seen the dead boy's face, looking up out of the dirt, his cheeks paler than the belly of a fish.

There was a saw-tooth knife in a leather pocket inside his boot. The younger brother slid this out and played a little five-finger with himself in the dust, moving the knife slow because of the dark and because there was nobody to see. The point of the knife went *thud, thud, thud*, punching into the dirt between his splayed fingers. Every so often he would pick his head up and look around; nothing moved in the desert. Once he thought he heard a coyote in the far distance, barking and laughing at the sliver moon. But mostly there was the sound of his knife and the sound of his breathing, and the great hush of wide-open spaces.

If he hadn't paused in his game to scratch his cheek with the side of the knife, he wouldn't have ever heard the sound. It came from right in front of him, and for a moment he couldn't place it. Then it came on again, louder this time: it was a stiff, whispering kind of sound. Under the curving moon, he could just make out the leather satchel on the ground. The satchel twitched—once, twice. The strange stiff sound creaked up again. It was the sound of bending leather. The satchel was opening, slowly, like a mouth with a stiff jaw.

The younger brother sat very still. The bag had stretched open as wide as it would go, open like the lips of a carp. It did not move again. He moved his hand slowly upward, feeling for the box of matches inside his shirt. He slid one free—just then came another sound, a strange tumbling noise this time, like the noise of a large stone rolling down a slope. He quickly struck the match against the heel of his boot and thrust it forward.

The leather satchel was turned on its side, drooping half-shut. But it was empty.

The young man lifted the match and sucked in a gasp. Now the pale, string-haired head was perched up on the crest of the rock, facing down toward him. The hair fell down the front of the rock like the roots of a tree. Its lips were still pulled back to show those perfect white teeth. And now the mouth had sagged open, the jaw sloping wider than a mouth should ever stretch. Inside he could see the tiny, dried tongue, like a pale bloodless worm cleaving to the jaws. As he watched, the eyelids flipped open, like a curtain yanking up before a show.

The young man called out in a hissing voice to his brother—twice, with no response.

Pain bit into his fingers; the match had burnt down, singeing the tips. He shook the flame out, and the world went full-dark once more. Quicky he reached for another—in that instant, the strange rolling stone-over-stone sound came again. In the light of the new match, there was nothing atop the jutting rock. The head was gone. In the desert, the darkness was enormous.

He swung the match left, then right. Its weak flicker lit up the ground only a few feet from him. Still nothing moved, and there was no more sound. His other hand closed on the grip of the knife. He called out again to his brother, but now his voice was only a strange dry whisper. He felt thick in his head, the same thickness the whiskey gave him. He felt like he was spinning. He glanced toward the creek bed. The match-light wouldn't reach that far.

From somewhere, anywhere, in the darkness, he heard the head rolling in the dust.

The young man said, so low only he could hear: "You shouldn't have said I was a half-wit."

He crept forward, holding the match above his head. When it burned out, the dark was another huge mouth, swallowing him whole.

Ø

One of the horses nickered—the older brother sat up straight from his bedroll, scrubbing at his eyes with one hand and reaching for the iron under his pillow with the other. He couldn't tell what time it was, or how long he'd slept. He pointed the gun up the slope, searching for movement. He heard the nervous slap-slap of the horses' reins, but nothing else stirred.

He called his brother's name, whispering between his teeth. No reply came. He muttered as he half-rose from his bedroll: "The half-wit's asleep. Found the whiskey again, more than likely."

Then his hand touched something beside him. His younger brother's head, facing away from him, stuck out the top of his own bedroll. He had touched the younger man's hair, stiff and sticky from sweat. He hissed at him: "Get up, good-for-nothing, somebody's snuck up on us..."

But his brother didn't stir. Didn't move. He reached out to shake him awake...

There was nothing at all inside the bedroll itself. The fresh slick gleam of blood showed under the crescent moon—and the young man's head rolled off the pillow, falling face-up in the dirt.

There wasn't time even to cry out. The horses both shrieked together; the older brother looked up in time to see it coming down the slope of the creek's bank toward him. It moved stiffly, taking quick jerky puppet-show steps, moving like it was wearing its boots backward. It had on his brother's duds, only now there was more blood dripping down from the collar and down his cotton shirtfront. It was the neck bleeding, just below the chin where his brother's—

His brother's head was lying in the dirt behind him.

It was the string-haired head perched on that bleeding stump of neck. Pale as paper still, with teeth bared and mouth sagging open. The creature juddered toward him; his brother's hands rose up, thrusting forward, twisting into claws. Under the weak moonlight, the older brother saw its open eyes, eyes with no expression or feeling.

He managed a scream at last, louder than the horses. He raised his arm, bringing the gun to bear, pulling the hammer back even as he aimed. He could not miss, not at that range, not even in that darkness. He squeezed the trigger—the gun barked again, and again, and again.

Each time, his aim was truer than a redskin's arrow.

His scream became a high hysterical laugh; it blew from him like the blast of a shotgun. The last shot, he could have pressed the gun right underneath its chin. He did—brain matter and skull flew skyward, dark against the paling sky. The expression on the pale thin face did not change an inch. And when cold strong hands closed around his throat, there was some guilty part inside of him that was grateful his brother's body still wouldn't fall.

Ø

The men had come out from Bitter Downs. There were three together, each on horseback. The man riding in front had the long gun balanced across his lap in the saddle; the two behind him shaded their eyes and bared their teeth at the hot wind. Three tin stars flashed late-morning sun.

The man with the long gun saw the camp first. He called out to the others, raising a closed fist over his head. His nag took the incline slowly, choosing her steps. He came up to the edge of the creek bed and stared down into it: there lay two bedrolls side by side and a loose pile that had been a fire sometime before. He called whoa to the nag and slid quietly down, moving toward the creek bank at a crouch, careful where he put his boots down. The stock of the long gun was snug into his shoulder. The other men rode up behind; each dismounted and moved forward with their hands on the irons slung through their belts.

The man with the long gun slipped down into the creek bed. First he poked at the bedrolls with the barrel of the gun; then he crouched, running his hands through the ashes of the old fire. Then he turned his face up, looking at the men who'd come with him. He said: "It's been cold a while. I figure the camp's abandoned."

One of the other men spat in the dirt. He said: "The brothers stole two horses from the wagon. I don't see two horses here. Maybe they saw us up on the ridge and bolted?"

The man with the long gun made a considering face. But something was eating at him. He turned back toward the bedrolls; the low hum sound he'd heard before grew louder and louder. The other two men with him saw him moving and left off talking. They watched as he lifted the long gun, poking the barrel under the flap of the nearest bedroll and lifting up—

A tremendous buzzing exploded upward. The man with the long gun stumbled back, nearly falling on his backside. Underneath the flap of the bedroll fairly squirmed with flies. They crawled thick and heavy, taking off and landing and taking off again, flying back in tight loops and shuffling over one another as they fed. Beneath them, it was all red fresh carrion.

Suddenly the men were shouting; for a time, it was difficult to tell who was talking.

"By God—that can't be them..."

"All the blood...all the blood..."

"The heads, what happened to the goddamned heads..."

One of the men turned smartly away from the creek bed, bent double, and emptied himself out in the dust. The man with the long gun pried back the other bedroll, then quickly let it fall again. He said: "It's the same under this one too."

"Would they do a thing like that? Redskins, I mean."

It was the man who had vomited talking, his voice thick as he wiped his mouth. The man with the long gun shrugged. He said slowly, without much confidence: "I guess they might."

The third man called out: "Colonel!"

He was up past where the man with the long gun could see; quickly he scrambled out, glad to put distance between himself and the two piles of crawling flies. The man who had shouted was near a tall jutting rock that came up at an angle from the dust. In his hands was a black leather satchel.

The man holding the long gun said: "That what was stolen?"

"I figure it was. Even redskins would take the money though, wouldn't they?"

"I figure they would. Where'd you find it?"

Weighing it in his hands, he said: "I found it right here. It feels full, kind of...heavy."

He made a motion to open the clasps; the man with the long gun waved his hand no. He said: "Let the next of kin do that. If any money's missing, I don't want them casting aspersions."

"What do we do with the..."

The other man's voice trailed off. What was in those bedrolls were not bodies. Again the man with the long gun shrugged his shoulders, making that same studied face. He said: "Leave them. Coyotes will come around sooner or later. The brothers had no kin in Bitter Downs anyhow."

Neither of the other two men moved. There was a feeling shared among them that coyotes, or even vultures, wouldn't touch the horror in that creek bed. They all looked at the man with the long gun expectantly. It was the man who had vomited who spoke:

"Colonel... What do you think happened here?"

The answer came back: "I guess they hit on some bad luck, is all. Same as them in the wagon."

The others looked at each other. This seemed like answer enough. The man holding the satchel spat once more in the dirt, kicking up a little dust. He said:

"Well—I reckon it couldn't have happened to a couple of nicer boys."

The rest of the men nodded assent. They were thinking of the fat man and his son, who would be buried in the evening the following day. One by one they mounted up and started the long ride back up the ridge and into town. Now the man with the long gun had the black satchel; it was fastened to his saddle, bouncing against his horse's flank just by his knee. The sun was at his back and getting hotter, pressing against his exposed neck.

He let the other two men ride ahead. The picture of the red pulpy flesh under the flaps of the bedrolls kept crowding into his mind. The featureless land offered no distraction; now he could also hear the flies, almost hear the sound of them chewing as they crawled and buzzed.

And there was something else. There by his knee—something had twitched. It had been only for a moment, but he was sure he'd felt it. Something inside the satchel, flexing slightly. His thoughts flew to rattlesnakes, scorpions. Nasty things found in the toe of a boot or curled in the foot-end of somebody's bedroll. He stared at the black satchel; the rhythm of its bouncing was the rhythm of his own heart. There was nothing out of the ordinary about it. But he was sure: only for an instant, but he'd felt something there. Something moving.

Something a little bigger than bad luck...

The long gun was slung over his back, leaving his hands free. If he reached down for the satchel, he would only have to take one hand off the reins, and only for a moment. He did not think of the red horror in the campsite again; his mind was a curious blank, like a sky with no clouds. The wind picked up and blew back in toward town, carrying no smell, no stink of blood. Just outside Bitter Downs, the riders were on the long sloping path going home.

Mister Mickenzie

I've never told this to anybody.

God's honest truth—I haven't. I don't even think about it privately anymore. I think that might call it all back. That might give it too much life. I don't want to breathe air into the balloon, see it bobble and twist and start to rise, feel the string go taut in my shaking hand.

But I don't want to forget either. Then nobody will be safe.

I'm writing this for the time coming later when the memory does fade. Maybe this won't keep me safe at all, but it might protect the children. Even when I forget it all and the balloon loses its air and lies limp, they might be kept clear.

No matter what else they've done—they deserve that much.

It's the only thing I have left to give.

Ø

Max and Libby are playing upstairs. That's how I remember it now.

I'm in the kitchen. The floor tiles are cold through my socks. My head's stuck in the fridge, rooting at the back for something. I can hear the muffled sound of their play over the fridge's quiet static hum. No laughter, just soft back-and-forth kiddie dialogue like you'd hear in a play. Max, followed by little Libby. Always in that order. Always call and response.

The clock over the stove said eight, or near enough to it. They'd begged me to stay up: "Five more minutes, Laura!" on to infinitum. And what the hell—I let them. They'd been good. They were always good. What was five more minutes of toy-time. They'd sleep in tomorrow and be back on schedule by the time their parents' plane touched down at the tail of the weekend. Plus: I remembered how hard it was to sleep in the summer when you're that small, when the sun never seems to set. When the sky stays bright well until after ten.

It was late July—I didn't know it yet, but that was the end of summer.

No August heat coming. No August coming at all.

Upstairs: suddenly I can't hear the children's voices. I can't hear anything. There's stillness in the big house. I call their names into empty silence. "Ma-aaax! Liiii-bby!" Playfulness stretches the syllables out. Something moves upstairs. Not the patter of small feet. Something big and heavy, getting dragged across the carpet.

I call out again. No answer—but the children start talking again. Their voices are hushed, talking in high little-girl whispers. I don't hear the heavy sound again. The fridge door is still open. I push it closed softly, still listening. The house seems huge around those whispers. I don't know why, but I creep silently to the bottom of the stairs, peering up where I know their playroom is. I lean out, putting one hand on the fourth step.

Does the upstairs look darker? Has a light burned out somewhere?

More silence. Then suddenly both sisters' voices cry out in chorus:

"Mister Mickenzie! Mister Mickenzie! Mister Mickenzie!"

I jump back, losing my balance. Crash against the hall door at the bottom of the stairs. The heavy brass knob digs into my ribs. Before I get my bearings, I hear it again. That heavy sliding sound. Something very big and very dense, being dragged over the carpet upstairs. The children start chanting again. Their voices mingle and crowd together. I can't make out the words now. It's in some child language I don't understand. Now I know for sure the upstairs hall is darker.

And it's three voices now, not two, getting louder and louder from the playroom.

$$\emptyset$$

I don't remember whose idea the gig was. Not at the start.

Best guess: my parents volunteered me, smelling blood in the water. A way to get me out of the house again. Really, the job felt like something pushed out of nothing-space. Like Arthur taking the sword from the lady in the lake, like something bestowed on me. But the Quarterfields were Mom and Dad's people, so they take all the credit. I hadn't met them before, formally: some rich couple my folks met at some church rally over the winter. I guess they all got along pretty famously, because I wound up sitting for their kids basically the entire summer. That's how my parents ran the ship back then. They sniffed something out, some job somebody needed done. I'd get drafted on a handshake. And because their friends were all "good church people," I was expected to dance when the music started and not bitch too much. That was all right, I guess. I bitched plenty, but that was before I heard about the money. Then I shut right the hell up.

Stan and Genevieve Quarterfield—the parents. The kids were sisters, Max and little Libby, nine and seven years old in that order. Stan was fortyish, I think. The mom was a little younger. Both with these lean, private-trainer bodies, the kind you'd order out of a magazine if you could. They were in business together; I don't know what exactly they sold, but they had to fly around a lot to sell it. As far as I could gather, they pretty much lived on jet airliners. Keynote speeches, conferences, high-stakes meetings in dark rooms, all of it. It meant they had to be able to leave at the drop of a hat. It meant they needed somebody like me.

They couldn't, or wouldn't, take their kids with them.

I never asked why. Back then, it didn't occur to me to ask questions.

The Quarterfields paid me up front at the start of June. One big check, with more zeroes on it than I'd ever seen before. That money bought my summer—all of it. I had to be on call whenever they had to ship off, for just as long as they needed me in the house. A deal like that meant I couldn't make long-range plans for my break, but by then I'd already made my mistakes with Reese. My social calendar was pretty much busted open. That part of the memory's already gone soft around the edges. I almost can't feel it anymore, even when I reach out for it. But I remember hurting bad enough that long days in some rich stranger's house seemed like some kind of escape. The money, and there was a lot of it, was just gravy.

That's God's honest truth too.

The Quarterfields could've hired some service to watch their brood. They could've scooped up any of a hundred other bored girls in my neighborhood. They picked me—or at least, I got picked. I said the money was gravy. But if you'd asked me back then what I'd do to get my hands on ten thou under the table, I guess I'd have told you just about anything.

Of course: if you asked me now, I don't know what I'd tell you.

I don't even know if I could answer at all.

Ø

We're in the motel now, all three of us. That's how I remember it now.

Little Libby's arms wrap around my thighs. I can see her reflection in the glass of the window, staring up at me with glassy eyes. She doesn't look scared, but her whole body's shaking against my legs. Max is on the bed, cross-legged, staring at the wall in front of her. Cold air rushes out of the AC unit beneath the window. A dull rattling howl baffles all noise coming in from outside the room. I feel my phone go off. I let it buzz until the caller quits.

Outside the window, the summer night is finally dark.

The parking lot's got four cars in it. One of them's my Sentra. The rest were there when we got here. A single tall streetlamp lights the whole lot, and moths gather like sharks around bait, striking and striking against it. Nothing else moves. The sky is clouding over, only showing slivers of moon through. The hum of the AC unit—it's hoarse and staccato. My nerves are on the tip of the razor. My brain is steel-wool fuzz, scraping in my skull.

For a flash, I forget the kids are in the room with me.

I'm thinking about the little plastic bottle in my purse. I'm thinking about the lead taste of fear that's pooling in my mouth. I'm thinking about a hundred other things.

Then the world snaps back. I hear Max's little toneless voice:

"When can we go back?"

"Just a few more minutes, sweetheart." My nose pushes against the window, trying to see farther into the dark. No headlights. No movement at all. It's near midnight now.

"I wanna see my daddy."

Libby now. I put my hand down at my side; she nuzzles into it.

"I just talked to him on the phone. He's coming to get you real soon."

"He doesn't know where to find us. He doesn't know about this place."

I look down at her and try to smile. "Your daddy's the one who said to wait here."

"Is he mad at us? For the candles?"

My heart squeezes. I sink down on my knees, taking her little face in my hands. "No—Libby, of course he's not mad at you. He's trying to protect you. And me too."

Max's voice is sullen from the bed: "He doesn't wanna go to the house. He knows we were playing the game. He knows Mister Mickenzie's there."

"I thought we agreed we wouldn't talk about that for a while."

"We broke the rules. You can't play the game halfway. Now Daddy's mad at us and Mister Mickenzie's mad at us and it's all your fault."

I almost don't look at her. I'm afraid of what I'd see sitting on the bed. A little girl—or something shaped like a little girl. But when I turn toward her, Max is crying into her dress. I put my arm out. She jumps down and joins her sister inside the hug. I pull both girls close to me, breathing them in. For a second I feel strong. I feel like an adult.

"You girls are being so brave," I tell them. "So, so brave."

Outside, long headlight beams swing into the parking lot.

I stand up, grabbing the girls' hands. I feel Libby and Max hesitate. It's only for a second, but I think they might fight against me. That they'd yank free and try to run. But when I tug their hands, they sniffle and follow me out the door and down the concrete stairs to the car.

Ø

I liked the Quarterfield children just fine. I liked the house even better.

The family lived in an old brick manor house, the kind that doesn't look right without ivy growing up the front wall. Inside was all sleek modern décor, but the façade had literary quality to it. A kind of old English charm. It looked like how a boarding school in a novel should look. It looked like something out of another age.

When I stayed overnight, I had my own guest bedroom with a bed twice the size of the one I slept in at home, with the softest white sheets I'd ever felt in my life. I could eat whatever food I found in the kitchen. I could shower in the big guest bath with hot water that never ran out, and the towels in the closet were just as soft as the sheets. When I got the kids to sleep I could watch TV or a movie on the big screen in the living room. Or if I had the patience I could set up the projector in the basement for surround sound. So long as Max and Libby were safe and fed and bathed and put in their pajamas on time, I could do just about anything I wanted in that big house. Sometimes I would just wander, losing myself in the maze of rooms, listening to the faraway sounds of the sisters playing elsewhere, in the playroom or back yard.

I didn't understand Max and little Libby at first. I'd never had younger siblings to compare them to, so I chalked it all up to inexperience. Libby seemed like your usual scab-kneed seven-year-old. But when she played with Max there came a change. They both seemed...muted, somehow. Running on emergency power. I can't explain it any clearer than that. They had their playroom upstairs, situated between their bedrooms, and I'd bring a book or my phone up to watch them with their toys. I'd sit in the rocking chair in the corner by the closet; they'd kneel on the carpet. Max took the lead in all their games. Even when they asked me to play with them, which didn't happen often, Max directed us, solemnly handing us specific toys or dolls and telling us which roles we would play. Libby didn't seem to mind. Or she never complained to me. But mostly they would play quietly on the floor in separate hemispheres. They acted out arcane pantomimes, speaking each doll's dialogue in soft voices and nodding their little heads.

All the kids I'd ever hung around before were noisy kids. I was a noisy kid myself. A screamer at the pool, at the park, shoving my big sister in the pews at Sunday Mass. But the Quarterfield sisters were quiet, always quiet. After a time, the quiet started to creep inside me somehow. I started to get funny ideas I couldn't shake. Watching the two of them playing together began to feel like watching a performance. I could imagine that when I left the playroom, Max and little Libby would freeze in their places, holding dolls or toy trains or stuffed animals. Or they would revert to some neutral pose, staring off into middle-space. They'd wait for me to return. They'd wait until they were being watched again. I imagined that when I came back, they might suddenly be in another part of the house, or someplace else altogether.

I imagined them watching me, even when I could not watch them.

But they were both such good-behaved little girls. Polite as well, unfailingly so, to each other as well as to me. Some sisters I know slap and pinch and holler when they get angry with the other, but I never saw anything like that between them. Only when Libby got something wrong in a game they were playing did I see Max take a stern note with her. I couldn't understand the nature of the transgression. Their games were so strange, the rules so remote even to my high school imagination. Once I took Libby aside. I asked her if she ever got to make up rules in any of the games. Her eyes got big and she shook her head hard. I remember how her braids slapped against the back of her head. Back and forth, back and forth. I asked her why she let Max make up all the games they played. Wouldn't she like to take the reins for a change? Wouldn't she like to be in charge for a little while?

But her eyes got bigger than before. Her face turned a wet-paper color.

She said Max didn't make up the games at all.

The games, she said, were all Mister Mickenzie's idea.

Ø

Something stirs—a memory from before. I'm panic-walking through the kitchen, the den, the hall. Then back through the kitchen again to start it over. I go around and around in a long, crooked loop like that, faster and faster. The children are upstairs playing.

It's my second week in the Quarterfield house.

That's how I remember it now.

I'm calling Reese again. Maybe it's inevitable. I watch my fingers hit the numbers on the screen like they're fixed to somebody else's hand. The call goes right to voicemail, but there's no way his phone is switched off. The second time, I try from the corded house phone. It sails through just fine. Three rings, then:

"H'lo?" It's a girl's voice answering. Not a voice I know, but definitely not Reese.

Gritted teeth don't hide the acid in my voice. "Who is this?"

"Huh?" In the background, I hear somebody else murmuring. The girl who answered says: "Shit, Reese—I think I've got your phone." Then comes a sleepy giggle from the other voice, Reese's voice, from somewhere else in the room.

I hold the phone away from my mouth, trying to get my breathing under control.

Steadily, I manage: "Put him on the phone, please."

"Who is it?"

Reese's voice in the background again. The other girl, I guess she just shrugs.

Then suddenly—a miracle. He's coming through loud and clear: "Laura?"

Oh God, my heart still kicks like a drum. Everything rushes up in me at once. All I want to say, it gets jammed in the door on the way out. All I can muster is: "Did you get the box I sent over? I left it with your brother. I wasn't sure when you would..."

Heavy breath into the phone. "Yeah. I got it."

"You sound exhausted. Are you sleeping any better?"

"Laura..."

"How's your arm?"

"Laura—stop it."

I pause, looking at the phone like I'll read his expression on the receiver. "Stop what?" A long cool stillness follows. I repeat the question: "Stop what? Reese, what are you saying?"

I hear his tinny sigh come through. "How're the new meds working out?"

"I don't know what you're talking about."

"Your mom told my mom. You don't have to lie to me anymore. It's all right."

There's a white-hot spot of light that flashes inside my skull. A pinprick of rage, shooting right behind my eyes. I want to go where he is. I want to drive to his mother's house, make him—somebody, anybody—eat that mote of pity I hear in his voice. Instead I breathe through my nose and twist my hair around my fist and say:

"They're working out fine. I'm fine."

"I guess you are. You sound mellower."

"So can I talk to you? I've had a good few months."

"We're talking now, yeah?"

I hear footsteps on the stairs. I sink down behind the counter; the phone cord follows me down. "I want to see you. I want to say I'm sorry."

"That's...not a good idea."

"You're not gonna let me apologize to you?"

"I'm still in PT. My leg's still sore where they took the stitches out."

"You still think I'm nuts." I try to breathe, in and out, in and out. "Reese—what did you tell them? At the hospital. You must have told them something."

"I told them I fell on the fork."

"So that's what happened."

For a moment, all I can hear is his breathing. I don't hear the girl in the background. Then he tells me, "All right, sure. That's what happened."

"So can I come talk to you? The kids' parents will be home tomorrow. I'll be free."

"Shit—I dunno. Can I think about it?"

Something claws inside me, something hungry and desperate. I have to choke it back. I have to stay calm, calm, calm, or everything will blow up again. Slowly the white-hot pinprick unknots inside my skull. Slowly I become myself again. I say, "Let's talk soon. I love you."

When I put the phone down, Max and Libby are peeking over the counter at me. Their eyes are huge and staring. When they look down at me, I wish I knew what they saw. I ask them, "You girls hungry for lunch yet?" and their little faces break open in gap-toothed smiles. But they don't stop staring. They never stop staring. I grunt and stand up, go to the cupboard, fetching down plates with cartoon flowers and princesses on them. Then I go to the silverware drawer. Everything inside glistens up at me, and I can finally smile.

Ø

Faster and faster, on into oblivion. When I tighten my grip, more details slip through the cracks in my fingers, gone forever. Maybe I should have told somebody, one more person to brace up against. Maybe then I wouldn't be floundering like I am now.

But no—this was the only path.

The only way to keep it all at bay. The only way to keep it sleeping.

My phone's buzzed twice while I've been writing this. I've been good. I haven't checked it, haven't even looked to see the number come up on the screen. I know better now than to fall into that careful trap. But I can feel it looming, lurking on the periphery. That feeling of being thrown into the shade, of a presence beyond myself. Let the children have their name for it. I won't speak it. I won't even take the call.

Maybe my writing all this is bringing it back to life.

But I am not the air in the balloon. I am the motherfucking pin.

Ø

Perhaps my first mistake was incuriosity. I never thought to ask any of the Quarterfields where the statue came from, or what it was for. Perhaps this was by design—the thing didn't match any of the manor house's décor, yet it never truly drew focus. At least I never thought of the statue as particularly strange. In the bright wash of glamor and wealth that was Max and little Lilly's lives, it barely distinguished itself from the backdrop.

You hear about natural camouflage. You hear about adaptation.

It was a brass statue, tremendously heavy. The shape was of a cartoonish butler wearing a black painted uniform with a white towel draped over one arm and a silver platter raised up on the opposite hand. The man's face was ruddy, with red circular cheeks and a smart black moustache and black wispy hair on the top of the head. The eyes were shut, creating an expression of bliss on the painted face—satisfaction in a job well done, I guess. The paint was chipped in places and stained from the children's fingerprints, because when either Lilly or Max would pass the statue, they would pat its head or run their hands across its face.

"Hello, Mister Mickenzie," they'd say, or, "Mister Mickenzie— so nice to see you again!"

They'd say this with affected British accents, of course, and hold their hands over their mouths and giggle. Or—Lilly might giggle. Solemn Max remained as stoic as always, and would greet the statue with a grave, drawn face. The name, of course, came from the brand: around the inner ring of the platter's surface, the words MICKENZIE COMPANY were stenciled into the metal, along with a trademarked symbol. This platter also had circular grooves in its surface, three forming a triangle in the center of the larger disc. These could hold something in place, I assumed, drinks or perhaps candles.

The statue was of a butler, after all. His function was to serve.

All these details come to me now, but I can't say I really registered them during my time in the Quarterfield house. A fear grows. I wonder—are these memories traps as well? I know my thoughts are not my own. I know I'm not safe. But surely my memories, formed before that night, can't be touched. Can't be grabbed and manipulated, like the limbs of one of Max's dolls. But there is no Mickenzie Company. And even though I've found butler statues similar to Mister Mickenzie, none quite match entirely. The pose is off by a degree, or the face is wrong, or the platter is too large or too small. The children loved him, of course—in the way only a child can love. Even their love for a toy is real, or something beyond a toy.

But the fear grows and grows.

I should not write more than this. I feel the trap closing all around now. The phone buzzes without stopping. I should throw it away, smash it under my heel. I should throw this story in a fire and watch to make sure it burns completely. But I do not want to forget. I'm afraid of that more than anything, even more than I'm afraid of Mister Mickenzie.

I can be strong a while longer.

There is more to come, much more. And I have so much more to say.

Ø

An addendum. I don't blame the Quarterfields for what came later.

At least—I can't put much blame on the parents. I didn't speak with them much, but they really seemed decent enough. They paid me well and treated me kindly. And they tried to safeguard their girls as best they could, clumsy though their efforts were. Clumsy and halting. They did not protect me. Perhaps they thought I'd be kept out of it. I can't speculate, or I choose not to. None of it makes any difference to me now.

But for the children's part: I can't make my mind up in one direction or the other. Seven is an innocent age. Maybe nine is too. But the girls weren't dumb. They reasoned just fine. So I can't call what happened later with them inadvertent. Everything was too finely laid out for that, too carefully orchestrated. They had a plan in play. The game had rules, even if they were only following them blindly.

Did they understand? In their hearts, did they grasp it all? Perhaps not.

Some things are so terrible they can only exist by chance.

But the other things, the worst things—they can never happen on accident.

Ø

The air suddenly becomes cold as I go up the stairs. I don't hear the AC turn on in the house, but I feel the blast, the sudden chill. The hall upstairs is darker. It's like the color has gotten halfway drunk out of the walls, the carpet, the air itself. The door into the playroom is shut. Max and Lilly, I can hear them chanting behind it, along with that third voice, deeper than theirs, deeper than any man's. Beneath the door, electric lights flicker like flames. The door has a chain, to be fastened from my side of the door. Somewhere, a dog starts barking desperately.

That's how I remember it now.

As I'm coming up to the door, there's sudden quiet on the other side. I push through as though into a dream. The room on the other side: dark, consuming dark, shrouded by the blackout curtains over the window, which faces the street. The only light comes from ten tiny candles arranged in a ring, all dripping wax onto the carpet. Max and little Lilly are in the ring's center. Lilly sits in the purple plastic chair from their play-table; it takes a moment of my eyes adjusting to see she's tied to it hand and foot, using what looks like jump rope. Max stands behind her. One hand is on her sister's shoulder. The other clutches a small plastic butcher's knife from the toy kitchen tucked in the corner of the room. The knife hasn't got any edge on it, it wouldn't cut butter. But Max has it raised in her fist with the point aimed downward at her sister's neck. It's this tableau I see as I first come through the door into the room. Both girls stop and stare at me with the biggest eyes. The flames around their feet light up only the bottoms of their faces. Their eyes, those huge eyes, stare out of darkness.

Outside the circle, facing toward the girls, the statue of the butler stands resolute.

He's beautiful in the candlelight. That's the thought that strikes first. His faded colors, his chipping paint, all rendered whole and gleaming by those flames. He's facing away from me, toward the girls. I see for the first time that on his backside, the coattails of his painted uniform are separate from the brass of his body and dangle independently, nearly touching the floor. Behind them are drag-marks, scuffed into the carpet leading toward the door, toward me. I can't see his face. I watch the girls' gaze sink from me, looking at Mister Mickenzie—I'm suddenly consumed by a notion that the statue's face has...changed. Not in expression, but that it's been replaced, altered at its core. As different from where it began as my face is from my mother's, from Reese's, from little Lilly's. The platter on the statue's outstretched palm is raised toward the girls, in a gesture of offering...

No, not in offering. The realization hits like a knife between my ribs.

Not an offering—a supplication. And on the platter's surface...

"Five more minutes, Laura," begs Max, her face solemn.

Lilly blinks up at me. She looks close to crying, but her voice holds steady.

"Yes, five more minutes. Please, Laura..."

I look from one face to the next. Words won't come; I'm shocked numb, like I've been drenched in icy water. Soon the cold will come, the cold or the fear. But now I'm calm and slow. I hold my hands out toward the girls. The smile on my face feels like it belongs to some other girl, because it does. Some other girl is driving. Somebody braver than me.

"No," this other girl says in my voice. "It's past your bedtimes."

Slowly, Max nods and pats her sister on the shoulder. She steps gingerly out of the circle of candles, coming toward me with the plastic knife. She presses it into my hand and pads out of the room behind me. Little Lilly shrugs out of her bonds easily. She stands, stretches her short legs, then crouches to the ground. I see she's going to blow the candles out—I have a sudden vision of the room plunged in total darkness. I imagine hearing things moving in that darkness, low dragging sounds and low dragging voices.

I say, "Leave those alone. I'll take care of them."

Lilly stands back up and hops out of the candle ring. Before she quits the room, I feel her arms wrap around my leg. She's little but she's strong, her grip crushing.

"I love you, Laura," she says. Then she's out in the hall with her sister.

Slowly I back toward the door. I don't blow the candles out. The numbness holds, but the fear claws at the edges, gnawing, scrambling for purchase. The open door bumps against my back. I squeeze past it, out into the hall. Lilly and Max are waiting at the top of the stairs, watching me. I think Lilly is crying a little. Max has her arm around her sister, their game from before forgotten. I look toward them and try to smile again.

From inside the room, the deep sliding sound comes scraping quickly toward me.

I slam the door shut. I must have screamed because my breathing is suddenly ragged, my throat all scraped up inside. My fingers scrabble on the playroom lock-chain. Finally the peg slides into its groove. Did something tap against the inside of the door? Something heavy, impossibly heavy, something two small girls could never move by themselves?

Had I heard something breathe behind the solid wood? A voice? A word?

I get the girls down the stairs. Out through the hall, out onto the front lawn. Lilly's got my hand tight in hers, almost leading me forward. In my other hand I'm dialing Stan Quarterfield. I almost dial 911, but something stops me. Some nameless thing inside me tells me these girls need their father. I look up at the front of the house. Between the blackout curtains, I can see the light from the candles flickering weakly. But I can't see beyond that, into the room. I can't see a brass statue still standing by a closed door, waiting for two children who are never coming back. The phone in my hand is ringing. I let it drop to my side. Max leans against me, her face rigid. The light in the playroom window has burned out. From my hand, I can hear Stan Quarterfield's voice calling out, "Hello? Laura? Hello?"

But it's like I'm lost in the dream, numb and calm and slow.

It's like I'm not even there at all.

The statue, Mister Mickenzie—it had turned around. The platter, upraised, had faced toward me, and the...thing laid out on its surface had squirmed slick and wet in the light from the hall. It had been closer. It had moved, dragged itself toward me about two feet. Perhaps that's all it could manage under its own power. I had interrupted it, stopped the game before it could begin. But it had moved. I had seen it, turning, coming straight toward me.

And the eyes on its painted face—they'd been open, wide open.

They'd been human eyes.

Ø

Getting near the end of my paper now. They only give me so much here. I guess I'm lucky they give me a pencil at all, considering. But I've still got enough light left to write by, and enough inside my head to fill a hundred reams. I can feel them watching me—through the cameras, through the bars. I know what they think they'll read when they take it from me, my story. I take no pleasure disappointing them. But I can't give them what they want. I can only give them the truth, whatever it might cost me. Let them hate me for it. The children are safe. The children are all I care about now.

I'll finish it—I'll finish it all.

I'll wear this pencil down to the nub.

I'll write on the wall. I'll write on my own skin.

In my own blood—if that's what it takes.

Ø

I talk with Stan Quarterfield for three minutes. That's how I remember it now.

He stays calm when I tell him about the statue. In the background, I hear him call out to somebody—some other name, and the woman who answers is not his wife. He listens silently when I tell him about the candles, the plastic knife, the sound of Mister Mickenzie sliding across the carpet toward me and battering against the door.

All he says is: "Christ—it came back. It came back."

Only then do I start to really understand.

He asks if I locked the playroom door, and he's glad when I tell him yes. He tells me to take the children, go to a motel. He gives me an address, a room number. Like he prepared this. Like there was a plan, a failsafe, all from the start. But I can hear the fearful undercurrent in his voice and know that's not true at all. He'll pay for the room, he says. Go there and wait with Max and little Lilly, and he'll come and pick them up. I'll be relieved of my duty to them after that, all of them. I'll have my summer back, what's left of it. There's a quaver in his voice when he tells me how grateful he is to me. But this feels forced somehow. His tone underneath is grim as stone. I ask him if he wants to talk to his girls, but he says there's not time. He'll be there soon enough, and I should get to the motel.

I hang up. I wonder, then, if Stan Quarterfield is afraid of his daughters.

Then I put it out of my head and bundle the girls into my car and start to drive.

The first call comes in a few minutes before we arrive at the motel. Mr. Quarterfield's name and face come up on the screen; I answer and stow the phone between my cheek and my shoulder, keeping my hands on the wheel. I don't even have time to say hello.

Stan Quarterfield says, "Where are my girls, Laura?"

A cold thrill raises every hair on my neck. "I'm sorry?"

"Where are you taking them? My girls—Max and Lilly. Where are they?"

It's his voice, really his voice. But there's something beneath it. A rumble, a vibration. I heard it before, at the house. I heard it in the playroom behind that locked door. The third voice, the deeper voice, chanting with the girls. It's there inside Mr. Quarterfield's voice, just beneath every word. Low and harsh—like brass scraping over carpeting.

"Where are my girls? You took them. Where are you going with them?"

I say, "You told me to take them. You told me where."

I'm crying suddenly. Now the fear breaks through and I'm crying. Max and little Lilly are in the back seat, buckled in and as quiet as ever. They'll hear the terror in my voice. I swallow hard, trying to cram the fright back down inside myself.

I say, "I don't understand." But I can barely get the words out.

"Come back to the house. I can get them from you there."

I picture the eyes of the statue, suddenly wet and blinking, real human eyes inside the painted brass face. Not fixed in the metal, but peering through, looking out from some other place. I imagine the voice on the phone coming out of those holes in the brass, reaching out to me across incredible distances—across the dark night, or the dark of space. The voice of something old and huge, something patient. Something that wanted the children.

But it didn't know where I was. It didn't know where I was going.

Into the phone I say, "You're not him. You'll never be him."

I hang up and toss the phone aside. That was the first call.

Ø

This is the second.

We arrive at the motel. We check in and wait. Sometime during that wait, I call Reese, or he calls me. Yes—I think I call him. That memory hasn't gone yet. My nerves are little live wires under my skin, humming high and thin. I have to talk to somebody, somebody who wasn't an adult and who wasn't a child. I call him, and on the second ring he answers.

That's how I remember it now.

I hear the line click open, and I don't even wait for him to talk. It all pours out: "Reese—thank God. I just had to...I just had to..." Then I'm blubbering. Words tumble over each other in a kind of soup. I can feel Max and Lilly staring at me with concerned eyes, but I can't stop myself. Reese is saying something I can't hear under the sound of my own voice.

"I'm sorry," I tell him. "I'm sorry, and you can send back the box if you want to. You were right. You were right, and your mom was right, and my mom was right. Everybody was goddamn right about me. But I don't care. Just...talk. Say anything at all. Talk to me about anything you want."

"All right," Reese says. "Tell me where my girls are, Laura."

For a moment, I stand very still, the phone still pressed to my ear. I can hear breathing on the end of the line—Reese's, and something beyond him. I hang up and I very carefully slip the phone into my purse. I think about the plastic bottle of the new pills in the purse next to the phone. I think about screaming. Instead I creep to the motel door and test the lock one more time. The room has a chain lock, just like the playroom door.

It only fastens from the inside.

Ø

Out of room now, and time. But I've got down enough. If they'll let me keep what I've written after they're through, I'll be able to cling together a good long while. Oh—they'll pore over it for sure. They'll pick me apart with my own words. Hidden meanings, code phrases, unconscious revelations. Anything to pin me. Anything to screw my guilt down tight. But it won't help them. They'll never find what they're looking for, these detectives.

This was never a confession.

This was barely a story. It's only how I remember it happening.

Soon that will slip away too.

But for now, it's a wall, a shield—to keep him out. The thing inside the statue. The thing that wore Stan Quarterfield's voice as a mask, to trap me, just like these detectives want to trap me. They both want the children, but Mister Mickenzie would win that footrace if I talked. He'd get to them first. He's old and he's patient, but he's not slow. What does distance mean to something like that? Without the masks, without the statue, he might as well already be there. But the detectives would never believe that. They haven't seen what I've seen.

I could never hurt those girls. But everybody keeps asking, asking, asking...

That means I'm winning, doesn't it? That Mister Mickenzie hasn't gotten them yet?

Where are they? I couldn't ever write that down, even if I knew the answer. Ask me where Stan and Genevieve Quarterfield are. I hope they're far away. Or, at least, far enough. They have the money to run a long time. But the detectives never ask me anything about the parents. Only the girls. And they ask about the fire—the fire that started in the playroom.

I hope Max and Lilly are safe. God's honest truth, I do. I hope they think about me, but in time I know they'll forget. What bliss, what peace. But I have to be careful. I don't have any illusions anymore. Someday, I'll make a mistake. That day's coming—when I'll slip up, when I'll forget. I'll let Mister Mickenzie in and lead him back to his girls. They can play their games forever. Bedtime never comes. Summer never ends.

That day will come. But not yet. Please, God—not yet.

I can hear the detectives coming back now. Just as well: this is the last of the paper. They'll take it from me, and maybe they won't give it back. I'll handle that as best I can, but first they'll try to sugar me up. They'll ask me if I'm comfortable. Too hot, too cold. They'll ask me if they can get me anything. And now I finally know what to ask for.

I'll tell them I want my purse. It's in evidence right now, but they'll get it for me if I ask. I don't want the phone charger that's buried in there, or the half-gone bottle of tiny white pills. I want to see what I brought here from the Quarterfield house. The *thing* I took from Mister Mickenzie's platter. I want to touch it, hold it in my hand. I want to feel it wet and slick and squirming. Then I can be satisfied. Then I'll know I saw everything I remember.

Then I'll tell them: I want a cell. And a door that locks from *both* sides.

"Five more minutes, Laura," begs Max, her face solemn.

1855

The following represents a verifiably accurate transcription of correspondence between a Mr. Timothy Ford in New York City and one Dr. Douglas Montebank at the University of Cambridge in Britain. Historical records indicate Ford was director of the New York City Foundling Institution at the date of postmark; Montebank was a tenured professor at Cambridge at that same time. While certain aspects of this account have been altered to protect the privacy of any still-living descendants of either correspondent, the narrative herein can be understood to be genuine in fact and detail and should be taken overall as a true accounting of events.

Addressed to
Dr. Douglas Montebank
University of Cambridge, Department of the Sciences
1 Trumpington Street, Cambridge, England
29 July 1855

My Dear Douglas,

Apologies first for the tardiness of this communication; the returning train from my younger cousin's wedding in Virginia was delayed inexplicably, leaving me without my luggage in Richmond for nearly four days. Then upon my return to New York, a new batch of arrivals immediately consumed my attention. The long and short of it is this: a brutal fire in one of the poorer neighborhoods on Long Island took nearly a mile square of tenements, the end result being nearly forty motherless children in need of care. The orphanage on the island itself had beds available for twenty-five; my own institution took the overflow, fourteen youngsters in all. I've included a news clipping regarding the fire with this letter, to peruse at your leisure.

These all being children from the same neighborhood, thirteen of the new group knew of each other, which helped them adjust more quickly to their new accommodations. The fourteenth, however, was not so fortunate. I should say straight off that these fourteen children arrived while I was still on the journey back to New York; it was the holy sisters in my employ who relayed the details of these early days to me. This last child was called Luca Palermo—dusky of skin and eyes and hair, like the Christ-child is depicted sometimes in paintings. Luca did not seem to know the other arrivals; in fact, in the few days before I arrived back, he failed to speak more than a few solemn words to anyone, as reported by Sister Marie-Francis. These were in heavily accented English: clearly the boy was an immigrant who had somehow been folded into the throng of orphan arrivals at my institute. Even two weeks after my return it was uncertain if Luca was truly an orphan at all, for none of the sisters nor myself spoke more than a dozen words between us of Italian—his native tongue, we discerned.

My friend, it is in the case of this mysterious young man that I would once more call upon your wise council. I have labored for two weeks to come to terms with the implications of the recent events at my institution and, over and over again, the well has come dry when I drop the bucket down in. I hope that your learning, or at the very least your keen intuition, will help me make some sense of this situation, and better still divine the best path forward.

I believe this Luca Palermo to be eight years old, or a little older. In the two weeks I have had to observe him, he interacted very little with either the sisters or myself, or even with the other children at my institution, many of whom were close to his own age. At first I reasoned that it must be the difficulty of language, coupled with the distress of losing his parents: how huge and lonely the world must seem, being unable to communicate except in fragments of a tongue not your own! Mostly Luca kept to himself, refusing to play with the other children when they were brought out to the courtyard, preferring to find a shaded corner with a toy or two and make his own small mischiefs there. I was concerned initially with thoughts to his education, but on the whole his quiet temperament meant that he escaped my notice for the most part; thus the true strangeness of his behavior did not ring its bell until after the first week or so.

Then came the night of 20 July—a Friday. I was asleep; it was again Sister Marie-Francis making the rounds in the boys' sleeping-quarters by light of a hooded lantern. I was later woken by a knock at the door of my own bedroom. Covering myself with a robe, I found the good sister in my doorway. I asked her what she could want at such a late hour, and my friend, I will never forget the cold righteous fear in her voice as she gave her reply:

"The boy, Luca Palermo—he speaks with the Devil."

I confess my own blood ran a little chilly at this, but it was more from the expression on her face in the lantern-light than from any true fear of a demonic force. I have told you in the past that I am lapsed in my faith—a point of some friction between myself and Marie-Francis and the other sisters who work under me. So she was not satisfied to simply deliver this news and let me sleep; before I could protest my incredulity, she took me firmly by the sleeve of my nightshirt and led me down the hall and up the stairs to where the boys sleep in their one big room. The door to the room had been left ajar; we crept through it, Marie-Francis still leading me by the shirtsleeve. I remember thinking to myself that if someone had spotted us going up the stairs together, they might have thought we were engaged in a tryst of some kind. But such thoughts fled me soon enough, when we arrived near Luca's bed.

Sister Marie-Francis had doused the lantern by this point, forcing us to navigate by touch in the darkness. We moved silently—both of us had spent enough time in that old building to know which boards creaked and which did not, and the snores of the other boys covered our steps as well. Luca's bunk was the bottom of a stack of three; there, in the weak moonlight from an unshrouded window, we could make out the shape of him, sitting up on the bed.

"Listen..." Sister Marie-Francis hissed through her teeth.

Confused, I did as I was asked. Luca had not heard us or noticed our presence. At first, I heard only snores and the sound of my own breathing. Then Luca spoke, in Italian as before:

"*Mamma... Quando torni?*"

Only then did I see the other figure sitting in the bed with him.

My breathing and my heartbeat both seemed to stop—but only for a moment. My eyes were still adjusting to the lack of the lantern, and presently I understood what I beheld. Luca had lumped the bedclothes into a kind of person-shape, with his pillow and clothing-bag underneath the blanket to give the thing structure. This form leaned against the wood crossbeams of the bed, seeming to recline— indeed, it appeared so person-like in the dark that I had been completely deceived, at least briefly. I understood the situation immediately, especially when I saw Luca embrace the blanket-shape. He had called it *"Mamma..."* decipherable in any tongue. Here was a boy in extraordinary torment, who could not express his wants or fears to any around him. He missed his mother, so he built one, here in the dark, to comfort him. Very well...so he was orphaned after all. In truth, I felt relieved, if only to have the matter settled in my mind.

Now it was my turn to lead Marie-Francis by the arm. I did not chastise her for waking me or for her foolish superstition—I only told her that we would need to take special care of Luca, and that finding someone to translate the boy's Italian had now become a marquis issue for the Institution. Perhaps Luca did have family we could return him to, such was my reasoning at that time. For her part, Sister Marie-Francis seemed much embarrassed by her mistake and went back to her chambers without another word on the subject. I returned to sleep immediately, again believing the matter for the moment settled.

My friend, how wrong I truly was. Our troubles were only beginning.

The next morning a fight broke out in the boys' sleeping quarters. This is not a rare occurrence: boys fight, it is what makes them boys. But this morning, it was Luca in the middle of the *fracas*. The sisters were completely unable to separate the two brawlers, so I was called in: immediately I saw them beside Luca's bunk, the dark-haired boy astride the other, beating him mercilessly with his fists. The other boy was bleeding from the nose and crying loudly, apologizing...to Luca's deaf ears, who of course did not speak English. His victim was also bleeding from a half-ring cut on his cheek; apparently, Luca had bitten him.

Luca kept screaming out this phrase: *"Mamma nascosta! L'hai uccisa!"*

Indeed, his blanket-mother was in a pile on the floor beside the bunks. Evidently, one of the other boys had destroyed Luca's creation, and the dark-eyed boy was taking his revenge. When I pulled him off the other boy, he turned his fists and feet on me, though he was small enough not to injure me much. I still could not communicate with him, so I merely held him aloft in my arms until he stopped thrashing. Soon after he went limp, crying weakly. I brought him to my office and locked him inside, intending to interview one or two of the other children to work out a chain of events, but soon Luca came alive again, dashing himself against the locked door with all his strength, again crying out: "*Mamma nascosta! Mamma nascosta!*"

I was baffled as to how to proceed at first. I have spanked several of the boys in the past for various infractions, but this seemed to me to be an unusual case—one where corporal punishment might work against my goals, rather than for them. But with no way to speak to Luca, I could devise no method of disciplining him. Eventually I conspired with Sister Marie-Francis to give the boy a sedative to keep him from injuring himself and left him dozing in my office while I consulted with her and a few of the other sisters regarding how best to proceed next. Marie-Francis again insisted on asserting the child's devil-connection; disturbingly, the other sisters nodded agreement at this, but I waved them off.

"Have we not helped troubled boys like this before?" I asked them. "Have we not seen the shock and hurt of losing one's parents, one's place in the world, stir such behavior in youths twice Luca's age? The trouble is that we cannot communicate with him; it has placed a screen between him and us, a screen through which only shadows are visible. You see the Devil in these shadows—I see another kind of torment. But disregarding what shape the darkness takes, we must find some way of shining light into it..."

I confess: My voice raised a little when I spoke these words, and the sisters were all cowed by them, save for Marie-Francis. The fear in their eyes, the zealous fury at this child...it frustrated and incensed me in a manner I cannot quite put to words. But the result at least was a productive one. Another of the sisters, Jeannette, announced timidly that she might know of a solution to our predicament: a priest she knew from a Massachusetts parish, Father Bessio, would be in the city in three days' time. It had not been his intention to visit the Foundling Institution for more than a few minutes, but surely if he knew the severity of the situation, he could be counted upon to lend whatever aid he could. I was much heartened by this news: this priest, Jeanette said, spoke both English and Italian fluently. With a translator aiding us, we could surely learn the source of Luca's torment, and set about to helping him at last.

The next three days passed slowly. There was no encore to Luca's fight with the other boy, but there was great tension in the air at all times wherever he went. The other boys gave him a considerable berth, wary of his fury. He spoke even less than he had when he first arrived, and ate noticeably less as well. The blanket-mother, this *"mamma nascosta,"* did not make another appearance, nor did Marie-Francis or any of the other sisters report that Luca was speaking with the Devil or any other entity; I suspected that Luca was disassembling his creation every morning before we awoke, returning her to the bedclothes as men return to the dust.

Then, on the third day, Father Bessio arrived. He was a younger man than I had expected. I had pictured in my head a gray-haired wraith, stooped with age with wispy brows and a mouth pulled down by the weight of heavy jowls. But here was a young soldier, lean and hard-eyed, with a close-cropped beard on his chin and no hat on his head. When he arrived at the door of the Institution, he made very little introduction for himself. He shook my hand, kissed Sister Marie-Francis chastely on the cheek, and stepped across the threshold like a doctor visiting the house of a dying man. He said to me, casting his eyes around the vestibule:

"Show me where you are keeping the boy, please."

His words were accented, though the slant of his vowels was not so pronounced as Luca's. I told him I would give him the use of my office to interview the boy; how he had known about Luca I could not say, perhaps Sister Marie-Francis had passed some message to him. To this he nodded gratefully and sat down on a bench in the vestibule to wait, staring resolutely at a painting on the wall. I went upstairs to retrieve Luca, who had napped through the mid-afternoon, as had become his custom in the past few days. I admit I was somewhat relieved to see that no blanket-mother loomed above his sleeping form when I woke him up. Since the arrival of the priest, the atmosphere inside the Foundling Institute had become much heavier, as if the air itself was thicker, more difficult to breathe.

My office has a desk and chair, as well as a low couch on which I will occasionally doze during hotter afternoons in the summer. Father Bessio was sitting in the chair when I arrived with Luca, the sisters trailing behind me like young chicks after a mother hen. I gestured to the sofa, and Luca sank down into it, his dark eyes wide and slightly dazed from sleep. The sisters and I crowded around the door while the man and the boy regarded each other a while—then Bessio stood suddenly, crossed the room, and closed and locked the door in our faces.

Immediately I shouted in protest; I was afraid, you see, that Sister Marie-Francis had made some secret arrangement with the priest, still believing that the boy communed with the Devil. I worried that Bessio might harm Luca or threaten him—or try to perform an exorcism, a gesture I still believed fruitless at this stage. But the sisters crowded around me, held me back from beating on the door with my fists. It was Marie-Francis who hissed in my ear:

"Let him work. Let him talk to the boy, he's come all this way..."

So in this method they mollified me. I resigned myself to listening at the keyhole like a schoolboy. Thus did the interview take on an almost mythic form, as though it were a record of some secret meeting between conspirators. This is what I heard through the solid wood, translated for me by Bessio and transcribed as best as I can remember:

Bessio began: *"Sapete chi sono?"* Do you know who I am?

To this Luca gave no response; either he nodded or shook his head.

The priest said, *"Mi chiamo Bessio, sono un prete. Sai perché sono qui?"* My name is Bessio, I am a priest. Do you know why I am here?

Again the boy did not speak; if Bessio was frustrated by this, he made no sign of it. He asked Luca, *"Come ti chiamano?"* What do they call you?

"Luca Palermo."

"E dove sono i tuoi genitori, Luca Palermo?" And where are your parents?

"Mamma è morta, è stato tanto tempo fa." Mamma is dead, it happened a long time ago.

"E tuo padre?" And your father?

Again there was a moment's silence. I pictured Luca's face screwing up, or his eyes averting, flickering along the ceiling. Father Bessio repeated his question; at last the boy said:

"*Andato.*" Gone. Bessio grunted in confusion at this.

"*Vuoi dire che è morto anche lui?*" Gone? You mean he is dead as well?

"*No—andato, solo andato.*" No—gone, only gone.

"*Dov'è andato?*" Where has he gone?

Luca's voice was very quiet when he responded, but even before the priest translated the words into English I felt a peculiar thrill squirm through me. He said:

"*La madre nascosta lo ha.*" The hidden mother has him.

I felt Sister Marie-Francis' sharp fingernails bite into my arm. Shaking free of her grasp, I pressed my ear to the wood, my nerves still singing. *The hidden mother.* Was this some reference to the Blessed Virgin, I wondered, or to the strange bedclothes-creation Luca seemed so preoccupied with? I considered that perhaps Father Bessio had not translated this last fragment accurately and was preparing to call through the door to ask for clarification. The good priest and I were of a mind, however; no sooner did I open my mouth than Bessio asked:

"*Cosa vuoi dire con questo? Chi è questa persona?*"

This Father Bessio did not translate immediately, but I took it to mean, "What do you mean? Who is this person?" And indeed, the next few minutes were spent convincing young Luca to divulge this information. I heard the springs of my office's sofa squeak; the boy was fidgeting nervously upon it, I could imagine him wringing his small hands in his lap. But at last, after much cajoling and gentle words from the priest, the story began to come out.

Luca spoke slowly at first, as though he were unused to it, but soon enough it was like a dam had burst inside of him. Several times Father Bessio implored him to slow down so that he might translate for his audience beyond the door, but even so much of the tale the priest had to relate to me after the telling was all over. Therefore, some details and phrasings in this account maybe be condensed or refracted through my own lens, but I have endeavored to transcribe the boy's words as accurately as I possibly could. In any case: a stranger or more haunting tale I have not heard outside of the campfire stories of our youth...outside, perhaps, of the peculiar encounters my father claimed to have experienced during his time at war.

You will think me mad for believing it, no doubt—at first. But I believe even a learned man like yourself will find skepticism in meager supply after the evidence I intend to present here, not including the physical reproduction I have included with the letter and newsclipping.

Luca's story begins as follows:

Mamma died when I was much younger, but I remember her. I remember her holding me in her arms, the smell of her perfume, the sound of her voice. She smelled like lilacs and her voice was like an angel's voice. We lived in a single large room above Pappa's studio, and when we came to America we lived in much the same way, only somebody else owned the studio Pappa worked in. I do not remember Italy, much the same way I cannot remember my mother's face.

The sickness took her when I was only three; before, Pappa had taken many photographs of Mamma in his studio, but when she was dead the pictures of her made him sad, and he burned them, all but one. I asked Pappa many times what Mamma looked like, and often his answers were quite different, as though he also could not remember. But one day he simply showed me.

From a box in the small trunk of all Mamma's things he pulled a photograph, but it was of me and not of Mamma. It was me as a baby, back in Sicily. I was wearing only a cloth and sitting on some sort of strange chair. The bottom where I sat looked like any chair, but the back was shaped strangely, like there was somebody inside it, hidden. It looked like a Samhain ghost wearing a sheet, only the sheet was patterned like a quilt and there were no holes for the eyes.

Pappa pointed with his finger and said, There is your mamma.

I did not understand at first, but Pappa explained that this was the fashion begun in faraway Britain, to photograph small babies without their parents present in the frame. But of course, babies do not like to sit still for long to be photographed, so photographers there devised a way for their mammas to hold them while remaining hidden in the developed picture...

Here, Father Bessio described Luca demonstrating this particular technique in photography. With great exuberance, the boy took the priest by the hand and pulled him from his chair, then took the blanket from my sofa and, sitting in the chair himself, draped the blanket across his body so that only his feet stuck out the bottom. He held a cushion in his lap, as though he were comforting an infant, like you see girls do with their dollies. He laughed and giggled at this game, but quickly grew somber, perhaps from the gloom under the cover of the fabric.

I thought at first Pappa was joking, but this was truly the only image he had of my mother. This was not fair—he could remember Mamma's face. He knew the color of her eyes, the length of her hair. But there was no changing it. Mamma under the blanket was the only Mamma I would know. It would have to be enough.

But soon I got an idea. Pappa did not own the American studio he worked in now, but I was allowed to wander around wherever I wanted. The other men who worked there knew me, and knew I was a good boy and would not touch anything. I knew the rules but I was going to have to break them to see my mamma. It was a slow day and the middle of summer. The man who owned the shop had also come from Italy, and was taking riposo in a chair in the corner of the work floor. There was another chair, a big lovely armchair, set in the middle of the floor from a job earlier in the week, and I had the blanket from my little cot and several bundles of clothes. It was enough to make myself a Mamma nascosta, a hidden mother, like in the photographs. I took the bundles of clothes and I shaped them up like a woman's shape on the armchair, then I covered it up with the blanket. It did not look much like the photograph of Mamma with me in her lap, but when I sprayed her lilac perfume on the blanket, it was like a magic trick.

There she was, under the blanket. My mamma, like I remembered her.

I crawled into Mamma's lap, and though the bundles of clothes could not move to hold me I imagined her arms cradling me, her angel's voice telling me how much she loved me and Pappa. My chest was so tight, I thought my heart was going to burst like a wine-presser stepping on grapes. I think I started crying because the man who owned the shop woke up and saw what I was doing. I thought surely he would beat me—for crying, and for moving his things around. But he was kind, and when I explained to him what I was trying to do he did not laugh at me. He told me to sit in Mamma's lap and he pulled his big camera and the wooden tripod into the middle of the floor. The man told me to smile, but when the flash of light came I squeezed my eyes shut and ruined the picture.

He said, it does not matter. Now I had a new photograph of Mamma and me. He patted my hair and told me he would give Pappa and me the photograph once it had been developed, which would only take a few days.

But three days passed and Jacopo, the man who owned the studio, did not approach my father or me. I became nervous; had I done something to offend him? I thought I had been very well-behaved, but sometimes Pappa says I make una peste of myself. I do not mean to but sometimes it happens anyhow. But on the fourth day Jacopo knocked on the door of our room; I could see on his face something was wrong, for he looked like there was a shadow over his eyes, even though it was the middle of the day and the sun was high and hot. He had something in his hand—the developed photograph. But he kept it turned away from me, and very close to his chest.

He looked at me, then Pappa, then me again. He said, I do not understand what's happened. I thought something must have gone wrong with the fluid, or the flash. But those do not explain it. Luca, please do not be upset...

He turned the photograph toward me. I thought again that something was the matter with the light, or that my eyes had clouded. I rubbed them and looked again. But the image remained the same. In the photograph: there I was, sitting on the big comfortable arm chair. But my face was blurred out, like somebody had smudged their thumb across the picture. And there was no second form behind me. Mamma nascosta, the hidden mother, she was not there.

I did not understand it. I thought I had done something wrong to make Mamma nascosta leave, but I did not want Pappa to see me cry either. So I told him and Jacapo I had to use the bathroom. I went in and shut the door; there I cried, though I did not know why I wept. I did not know Mamma. And Mamma nascosta, she was only bundles of clothes under a blanket, scented with perfume. She was not a woman and could not, did not, love me.

Jacopo let me keep the photograph with my blurry face. I put it above the mantle but eventually looking at it every day began to make me sad, like the pictures of Mamma would make Pappa sad. So I brought it into the bedroom and put it under the pillow on my cot. Then a week went by, and...

At this juncture, I must interject to tell you that Luca broke off talking and apparently refused to continue for several moments. The priest, Bessio, reported that during this time the boy squeezed his eyes shut and lay back on the sofa, making small animal-like grunts whenever the priest asked him to speak or talked to him at all; he even twitched as though caught in some kind of tantrum, but this subsided as Bessio began to pray quickly over him in a quiet strong voice—soon Luca opened his eyes again and proceeded as though nothing at all had changed.

I felt the eyes of Sister Marie-Francis on me, pushing into me like the force of the wind. I would not look at her. I knew what she was thinking, just as somehow, in some secret arcane part of myself, I knew what must come next. Luca went on:

Then it was a week later. Pappa had become withdrawn again, as he does sometimes. Work was slow in the studio and there was not as much money for us; Pappa would sometimes spend what little we had on wine, which he said would help him with his sadness but only made him sadder most of the time.

But this time something was different. For two days he did not work, though it was the middle of the work week. He didn't move from his chair except to fetch more wine; I did not know where he got the bottles, there were so many. While he drank, he stared at a space above the window. I noticed on the second day that he had taken the photograph of Mamma and me and balanced it above the fireplace. His face was like a great red storm, and his eyes had clouds in them. Soon he would not even leave the chair at all and made me bring the wine to him. He would not pour it into a glass, but drink it from the bottle. The empty bottles piled all around him. And then—

Once more Luca broke off talking very briefly. Through the door I could hear the sound of his low sobs; my dear Douglas, it was all I could do to stop myself storming through into my office and sweeping the child up in my arms. You know I have a tender heart; it is a blessing and curse both in my occupation. But I held firm, and let this Bessio comfort the boy instead. He managed the trick, enough for Luca to say:

—and then on the second evening, I moved too slowly with a fresh full bottle for Pappa; something twitched and changed in his face and his fist came out and struck me on the side of the head. I fell sideways but I did not drop the bottle. Not a drop of the wine spilled. And I did not cry. I was too scared to cry, scared that if I wept I would be beaten harder. From the floor I looked up at Pappa—but Pappa was crying now, his red face down in his hands, his strong shoulders shaking.

I did not understand. I stood up, but I was still wary of him and did not move closer. Through his hands he was saying, Mio cuore, mi dispiace tanto... My heart, I am sorry. But he had never addressed me this way. When he picked his face out of his hands, I realized he was speaking not to me but to the picture of Mamma and me on the mantel. Sono rovinato, he said. Ho rovinato tutto...

I still did not understand. But before I could put aside my fear and ask him what he meant by it, I heard a sound coming from the space where we made our beds. It was a fluttering sound—like blankets or sheets on wash day, flapping on a drying line in a strong wind. It was like a great bird's wings beating the air. The noise came up suddenly toward us; I shut my eyes tight, and Pappa turned toward the sound, already crying out some foul word in a loud voice...

Then—suddenly he was quiet.

I opened my eyes. My father had fallen over sideways in the chair, nearly falling onto the floor. But I could not see him. Somehow the blankets from my bed were covering him now, head to foot so that no part of him showed underneath. He was not like Mamma nascosta; he was hardly shaped like a man at all beneath. I could see him moving slightly under the blanket, like a fly moves when caught in a spider's web. And strange noises came through the blanket, muffled and wet and soft as though they came from a great distance away.

I crept forward. My heart was like thunder in my ears. I was scared, but I did not understand why I was scared. I thought perhaps it was some child's game, that I would draw the cover away and my father would emerge, smiling, and tell me somehow that it had all been a game. But he was not moving. And those noises from under the blanket were growing louder. I stretched out my hand, reaching for the corner of the fabric, intent to tear the bedclothes off in one motion.

But I became too frightened. Suddenly I was imagining what I would see when the cover was removed. My mind was full of terrible pictures, but the worst was the idea that I would draw back the blanket and there would be nothing beneath at all, that I had made Pappa disappear like a stage magician's cabinet. So I crept to the corner of the room where our beds were kept and pressed my face into Pappa's pillow, facing away from the chair and the rest of the room.

I stayed there for a long time. Behind me, the strange wet noises from beneath my blanket rose and fell like a foghorn's voice. Once I thought I heard Pappa call out my name—but the sound was so quiet, and seemed to come from such a long way away that I was sure I imagined it. Eventually the room was silent again.

I lifted my head. My face was wet, my cheeks sticky from crying and from a little blood that had come from my nose when Pappa struck his blow. I turned toward the center of the room. There was the chair, and the scattered empty wine bottles. But the photograph was vanished from the mantelpiece. And Pappa was gone.

Sister Marie-Francis' fingernails dug sharply into me. I hardly felt the pain; my skin had gone cold all over, cold and numb. But still my heart remained as stone to the truth. Still I was unconvinced. Still I remained a non-believer. Luca needed no prompting from Bessio now; his voice held level as a carpenter's hand, speaking faster and faster now, tight in the grip of some other strange and terrible power...

> The blanket was still there, showing the shape of the chair under it. But there was nobody beneath. Outside the window, the streets had grown darker. Night was coming; even in our little room the shadows were long. I went over to the chair slowly. I was still wary, even if really I had no cause to be. I touched the rough surface of the wool blanket. It was as I remembered it. It did not jerk out of my grip or twitch in my hand. I pulled it away, and nothing lay beneath it. Pappa was nowhere. I was alone in that room, all alone.
>
> But—I would not be alone there for much longer.
>
> I took the blanket back to the bed. I was tired from crying and it was already late. I threw myself down, but I had no more tears in me. I had no feeling in me. Pappa was gone. He had crept out while I was crying, ashamed of me. I rolled over on my back on the bed, like this—but then, there was another weight pressing down beside me. In the dark, I saw a shape. I felt movement. Weight shifted on the bed. The shape was tall and dark and almost formless, like laundry on the line. But I was only afraid a moment. She smelled of lilacs. My mamma's perfume. And when she spoke it was in my mother's angel voice, low and sweet.
>
> I whispered, daring to hope, Mamma nascosta?
>
> It was. I rose and moved toward her on the bed. She gathered me up. Her arms, covered up by the blanket, were so strong. But her embrace was soft and gentle, just like my memories. The smell of lilac was all around me. We rocked back and forth, and the lullaby Mamma nascosta sang was so beautiful even if I did not understand any of the words. Inglese, like the man and these holy sisters speak, Signore Ford and the others. But she could speak to me, and in a way I could understand. I asked if she loved me:
>
> "Sì, cuore. Certo che ti amo." Yes, my heart, of course I love you.

I asked if she would leave, if I would be alone again.

"No—tu sei mio, e io sono tuo." No—you are mine, and I am yours.

This was enough. Her smell, her arms around me. The words she spoke. It should have been enough to satisfy me. But I had one more question in my heart.

"Dov'è papà, per favore dimmi...?" Where is Pappa? Please, tell me...

At this, Mamma nascosta bent herself above me; the blanket wrapped around me tightly. The smell of lilac was so strong then in my nose, and I could feel cold breath touch my cheek as the wool rubbed against my face.

She gave me her answer, and I was satisfied:

"Nessuno ci farà mai più del male." Nobody will hurt us ever again.

I slept like that, wrapped in Mamma nascosta's warm embrace. Then like another magic trick it was light—and I smelled smoke, and there was screaming and sirens outside, and Jacopo pounding the door yelling, Signore Palermo, Luca, come out, come out, there is a fire burning, the whole building will go. I ran outside quickly—by then Jacopo was gone, knocking on some other door. There was a large crowd in the street and I was swept away. All down the street I could smell smoke. Mamma nascosta remained behind; I did not see her again.

Now I am here, talking with you. That is all, and no more.

Father Bessio asked Luca a few more questions after this, but nothing much came of it. I will spare you the boredom of those details and leave you with the meat and gristle I have already imparted. Only then did Sister Marie-Francis let me through to confront Luca and the priest. The boy had moved back to the sofa and lay on his back there, watching me come through into the office with the corners of his eyes. He was flushed and panting; the telling of his story seemed to have taken some toll on him. But when I told him, Go upstairs to your bunk, let me talk with Father Bessio a while, he was calm as he trodded past me out the door. Bessio himself patted the boy's shoulder fondly as he passed him by but did not speak to him again. He crossed his arms behind him and waited to hear me speak.

I asked him, "Well—what can you tell us?" and he looked at me with a very serious expression, but there was some faraway quality to his eyes as well, as though he were a chessman thinking three, four, five moves ahead of the present.

"I have secured a room nearby," he said, and pressed a scrap of paper into my hand. "Call on me at this address if the situation worsens—or if anything new should develop. I will return to my quarters and write immediately to Rome. Goodbye, my friend."

This is all he would say. He bade Sister Marie-Francis goodbye, and shook my hand once more. His strong hand only shook slightly in my grasp; that told me more than his words could. Then the young soldier was gone, and I was left alone with the sisters, crowding around my office door, looking at me with identical pairs of round staring eyes.

I tell a lie—I was not alone in that office. Luca had left something in my chair for me, the heap of blankets and pillows he had used to describe this "Mamma nascosta" to Bessio, and by proxy to me. There was hardly a shape to this mound; I could make out the barest suggestion of a head, tilted to the side just slightly, and maybe some piece of a right shoulder. No more than that. But in the air, I thought... My dear Douglas, will you believe me if I tell you—

I smelled lilacs. Only for an instant, and then the sweet scent was gone.

I turned back to the heap of blankets and pillows on the chair. She was no more a woman-shape then she had been before. I shook myself; it was a boy's imagination and nothing more. A delusion, born out of grief at losing a mother too young and a father to some drunken misadventure—and a home to a terrible fire as well. Yet despite this, a peculiar childish urge siezed hold of me then. As the sisters watched, silent, from the doorsill, I went to the chair and rearranged the cushions and blankets with my hands; like a sculptor, I shaped and molded and stacked until I had created a better effigy of a woman sitting upright, facing out into the room, staring blankly out of an eyeless face.

I said to Sister Marie-Francis, "Fetch my camera, please. And the tripod."

Now we come to the reason I must write you this way, my friend. Marie-Francis looked as though she might protest; instead she padded away silently, returning only moments later with the boxy camera in her arms and the black darkcloth slung over her shoulder. Another sister trotted behind her, bearing the folded tripod legs. They flashed me severe blue glares but assisted me in setting up the apparatus, and only shared between them the slightest exasperated look when I bade them point the lens at the chair and positioned myself in the blanket-woman's lap. It might have made a peculiar keepsake, I think. Something to show my wife and children someday if I should ever marry and father children.

But instead I am sending the developed photograph to you, along with this letter and the other materials I have gathered. I told you I was lapsed in my faith. I had that lapse shaken in me that day, shaken in my very bones. It was not the boy Luca's story that accomplished this, nor was it the priest Bessio or the ministrations of the sisters. No, I am convinced that there must be an Almighty seated in the throne of Heaven, simply because there must be a throne of Heaven just as their is a seat equal in the frigid bowel of Hell. I say this because, in the moment of the camera's powder-flash, for a brief terrible instant—

Douglas... I saw the Devil.

Nobody saw it but me. The flash was too bright, or the movement too subtle or too swift. But as the powder exploded and filled the office with light, the head of the blanket-woman, the hidden mother, turned its featureless face toward me. And although there was no voice to sing them, I heard words, the beginning of a lullaby, a song of comfort in my head. But they were not in English as Luca had described. They were in no language I could place. Perhaps they were not in a language at all. Perhaps they were not words.

I leapt up from that chair as though I had been burned, upsetting the blankets behind me, sending the chair clattering to the floor of my office. The hidden mother scattered, returning to bedclothes. The sisters cried out in alarm and called out to me as I fled the room, but I did not respond to their pleas to return. I soon found myself in the Institute's courtyard, red-faced and sweating in the sun, collapsed against a low stone wall. The voice that was not a voice did not pursue me. Neither did the scent of lilac. I calmed myself and fixed the drape of my suitcoat and returned to work, but I could not return fully. I jump at shadows and sudden movements in the corner of my eye, loud noises or unexpected greetings. Grateful for the hot summer nights, I sleep without bedclothes entirely, wary of looming shapes appearing, built of blankets and quilts and pillows, rising and twisting in the darkness. And I barely speak to Luca Palermo.

Father Bessio did not return. Two days ago I visited the address he had provided; the landlord said the priest had vanished, leaving a small but significant unpaid tenancy. This I paid, not knowing what else to do. Now I am left with nothing but questions and the most pervasive sense of cold creeping dread. The sisters whisper behind their hands and stare at me when my back is turned. I walk the halls of my Institute now as though the mark of Cain burns on my brow. And what is far worse—whatever plagues or blesses Luca Palermo has spread like a queer sickness among the other boys. Any given night I can creep through their sleeping quarters and find a dozen, two dozen, two score of beds with the bedclothes piled up at the foot of the mattress, watchful sentinels all twisting toward me in the darkness. And if the lads are awake, I hear them whisper. I hear them address these shapes with one voice:

"*Mamma nascosta—portami a casa...*"

Hidden mother—take me home...

My dear Douglas, you are my oldest and most learned friend. I should have relied on your intellect from the very beginning; not doing so was my foolishness. That, or it was pride that kept me from your doorstep. Now yours is the only shelter I can turn to, and I hope I am not too late to escape the coming deluge. I feel it coming, just as surely as I smelt lilacs in my office that day. Just as surely as I saw the face of comfort and terror both turn toward me in a camera's flash. Just as surely as Luca Palermo's wine-dark eyes haunt me everywhere. So I come to you with a plea, and a desperate one. Tell me my anxiousness is irrational, unscientific. Tell me what I fear is mere delusion born of stress or hysteria or worse.

As promised, I have included all available physical evidence with this correspondence. Study them at your liesure; they are yours to keep. But I beg you: write back with all available haste. I have become a desperate man, and I am not used to desperation.

Help me to untie the knot I feel tightening at my neck. Help me unravel this tangle.

With your books and facts—explain away the nightmare I have dragged into my life.

Yours Most Modestly,

Timothy

Timothy Ford *was reported missing by his employees at the Foundling Institute on 3 August 1855; Dr. Douglass Montebank was last seen publicly 17 August the same year, vanishing soon after without a trace. The preceding letter was discovered in his office at Cambridge after his disappearance, laying opened on his desk. Included with the missive was the news clipping described, as well as a single developed photograph complete with photonegative. This image depicts a man of Ford's age and build with his face blurred or smudged, making positive identification impossible even with modern equipment and techniques.*

There is no second figure in the image.

According to historical records, neither sender nor recipient was ever seen again.

𝕬 𝕽𝖊𝖆𝖑 𝕷𝖎𝖐𝖊𝖓𝖊𝖘𝖘

I bet I'm calm enough to talk now. I don't know if I'll get through it, but I'm going to steam on ahead like I'll make it all the way. I'm not even sure if you'll believe what I'm going to tell you, but I've gotta tell *somebody*, Marshall—or it'll explode out of me, I swear it will.

First thing is: I've quit art school. Quit it whole hog. Broke my brushes and poured the paints out in the toilet. Dad's going to throw a fit, but I can face him. Mom too. I'm not afraid of them. I'll pay back the tuition money somehow. I'll work evenings, sell blood plasma. Whatever guys our age do for extra money these days.

But I'm not going back there. And I'm never picking up a paintbrush again.

I know how that sounds. My dad, he'd say I never knew what I wanted to do with my life. Mom would tell me that's not the kind of decision you can make in one night. But they're just protecting their investments. There are five or six moments, I think, in every guy's life...steering moments, where you've got to thrust the paddle down in the water and turn your boat one way or the other. *Which* way doesn't matter—but you've got to turn or the whole mess'll smash on the rocks. And once you've made that left-or-right choice, the whole river changes. The arc, the trajectory your life will take, is different. And even if you could see the other path, you couldn't get back on it, no matter how small the jump might look.

I've had one of those moments. A steering moment.

I hope to God it's my last for a long time.

Keep that bottle handy, please. I said I'm calm enough to talk, but I don't know how much longer that'll hold. And I don't want to spook you, but there's one more favor I'd like to ask before I start. That mirror on your door... Could you take it down and put it somewhere? In a closet maybe, or just facing the wall... There, yes, that's just fine. Sorry again for the hassle. I don't know where my head's at. I can't control my thoughts at all.

Shaking? You're damn right, I'm shaking. Like a leaf on a tree. I'm terrified, Marshall. I'm more scared than I've ever been in my whole life—but not *for* my life. Never for my life. I'm not in any danger, not anymore. But there are other kinds of terror, I'm learning.

Other kinds—*worse* kinds. And worse things to fear besides death.

Now pass me that bottle, and I'll tell you everything...

Ø

This started three days ago. Friday...late in the day before the weekend got going. My last class had let out hours ago, and I was walking through the gallery in the Jim Dublin Building with a half-finished painting under my arm, wrapped in brown paper for the trip home. The building had emptied. The only lights left on were in the main passageway, leaving the rest of the halls dim and quiet. My shoes slapped the tiles, echoing in the near-dark, and I was thinking about supper. So far as I knew, I was the only student left in the whole south quarter of campus.

But when I rounded the corner near the door leading out to the center walk, there was somebody else in the hall. I saw him from the back, standing by the wall between the bathrooms. He was younger than you or me—a freshman, I'd guess, with a red hoodie jacket and a pile of wavy hair balanced on the top of his head and a scruff of hair fixed to the point of his chin. There was a glass display case set in the wall, and he was facing it, leaning forward to peer through at the art hung up inside. There's something of mine hanging there now, a project from earlier in the semester. I could tell immediately, somehow, that he was looking at it through the glass. That's not vanity—I could *feel* it, Marshall, almost a physical sensation. A kind of prickling, like the pressure of eyes against your back. I could tell he was looking at my painting in that display case as surely as if I'd seen his eyes myself.

I was going to walk right past him. I'm not one of those artists who stands next to their own work when it's on display, waiting for someone to come up and ask whose it is. But I did want to know for certain it was my piece he was looking at. *That's* vanity—after all, I was only half-sure, feeling or no feeling. So as I neared the door, I let my eyes slip sideways without slowing, not even turning my head. That's when the other student spoke:

"It doesn't much look like her, does it?"

At first, I wasn't certain I'd heard him right. His voice was almost a whisper, and I thought for an instant he was talking to himself. But then he repeated himself, slightly louder, and as I turned my head toward him, I caught a flash of his reflection in the glass. He was looking straight at me.

"It doesn't look much like her at *all*..."

I stopped. It seemed impolite not to. Or perhaps I was already put under the spell. I know, now, that I should have been scared. But at the time, I can remember only a brief disquiet running through me, as though it was me who'd been caught staring. He only held my gaze for an instant; then his eyes refocused and he was looking through the glass once more. I thought I had seen a dull flash of a grin in the glass, but this was only a trick of the light.

Before we go any further, I want to tell you about that painting of mine hanging in that glass case, if only because you'll never see it yourself. I already said I'm not going back to the Dublin Building, and in fact I've emailed my fine arts professor, asking her to have it destroyed. I did that right before I came to see you. But it's important to me that you understand: This was just an ordinary painting. Only acrylic on canvas, nothing more. I'm not ashamed to admit that it wasn't really very good at all.

The painting was a portrait. *Unfinished Daydream*, I called it, a pretentious name for something I'd based on a scribble on lined paper I'd done during a Civics class. The subject was another student, a girl seated one row up from me in that same class. In the painting, she's sitting with her back to you, upright with her hair tucked down into the hood of her sweatshirt, her chin angled down and her brow in a line. Her head is hardly turned at all, so you can barely see her face—only the vague curve of her cheek and the crinkle of one eye. If I'm being honest, the likeness isn't very good, and it wasn't much better in the original sketch. And the expression I called a "daydream" could be cramps if you squinted at it.

I don't like drawing people from life. I hate staring at faces. I get self-conscious. When you stare at somebody, they stare back, and the act of drawing them becomes an act for their pleasure. It becomes a *performance*. Their expressions change, have you seen this? Their faces go slack sometimes, like they're watching television—but more often than not, they become masks. They are performing too, you see. You might as well just take a photograph, because the paintings will never show their real likenesses. Only their posing, their preening smiles. That's why I draw from candid photographs, or from memory. And I paint based on these sketches. The likenesses still aren't any good, but I like to think the essence, the character of the face, remains somehow. Maybe that's vanity too.

But I can tell you that *Unfinished Daydream* was different, even if there was nothing outwardly remarkable about my subject. But the instant she turned her head to the left, I got this strange notion that this was somehow a unique moment—unique entirely in its *un-uniqueness*, its un-beauty. A slab of life at its most torpid and mundane. And yet, I still don't know what compelled me to draw her. It was not, let's say, a conscious decision. My pencil moved almost without my ordering it, but I was also utterly absorbed by my task. I sketched in total silence, unaffected by the drone of the lecturer, never once taking my eyes off her shoulders and the pale crescent of her face.

Her face—yes! I think that's what attracted me. Not the beauty of her features but the simple fact that *I could not see them*. There was only that suggestion, that hint of expression. But that hint betrayed nothing, and therefore was less a face than if she'd had no face at all. The uncertainty of her expression destroyed all identity. She could have been happy or sad, ugly or lovely, female or male. A Schrodinger's face, neither living nor dead. I found myself enchanted by that idea—so I drew, nearly without blinking, in some strange and awesome frenzy...

And yet, when I'd finished, I felt nothing. No wave of satisfaction washed over me. The drawing in my hands was only a drawing. I don't know whether the girl knew I was sketching her, but she'd sat completely still for ten minutes, just long enough for me to finish my work. Then the bell rang and she scuttled out the door. I didn't see her again for nearly the rest of the semester. I'm not certain she was even enrolled in that class at all. I didn't even know her name.

The male student turned away from the glass, and for the first time I saw his whole face. A thin, hungry face, with no facial hair save for the scruff of goatee on his chin. His expression was serious, almost studying, and as he looked at me across that dark hallway, I could feel again a prickling on the backs of my arms. I clutched the canvas I held to my chest involuntarily, but at once eased it back to my side, feeling foolish.

"Do I know you?" I could think of nothing else to say.

"No, it's not a good likeness," the other boy said as though I hadn't spoken. "But that makes sense. You don't *know* her. How could you hope to capture her if you don't *know* her?"

I wondered, again, if he was talking to himself, but dismissed the idea. He hadn't taken his eyes off me. I glanced toward the door. Light filtered in through the crack between the doors and through the narrow windows set in each. It would be dark out soon. I want you to understand, I wasn't afraid of him then. I'm not a big person, but I got in enough fights as a kid that I know how to handle myself. And this other guy, he just wasn't giving off that air. Some guys, you can smell it on them. But this was just a kid. Harmless in an obvious kind of way.

But I had to reply somehow. "I don't understand," I told him, gesturing with my free arm to the glass behind his shoulder. "Do you know who she is?"

To my surprise, a laugh sprang out of him—a rolling, bleating kind of laugh, like a billy goat. "Do I know her?" he said once he had himself under control. "Do I know her?" He wiped his eyes on his sleeve and straightened, taking a few steps toward me.

"She's not for you to know," he continued. "I've had a little time to think about it, and I don't like the idea of you just staring at her for that long. But I suppose that damage is done. And to be fair, I've wanted something like this for a long time. A real likeness of her. Something that shows the real her, the way I see her. You've helped me realize that."

"You're welcome..." I replied. And then, almost in afterthought, I blurted, "I take commissions!" even though I've never done anything of the kind. But I had to say something. I still wasn't scared, but I didn't like the way this boy talked.

Again, that peculiar laugh rang out. "I'm sure you don't," he replied. "At any rate, you can't do what I need you to do. Not yet. Not quite."

I should have run, Marshall. That's all I've been able to think about these last few days. How I should have run in that moment. I should have dropped the canvas to the ground and burst through those double doors like a bat out of hell. But I did nothing. I stood there and did nothing.

"You just need to see her how I see her," the other boy told me.

Then he strode quickly across the hall and seized hold of my wrist—and almost immediately I felt myself slipping away...

Ø

The next half hour blazed by in a muddled, feverish blur. I recall, faintly, tucking my canvas beneath my arm and pushing through the double doors into the cold. I remember putting the key in the ignition of my car, but I don't remember how I got inside it. And I don't recall a second of the drive home. I simply arrived there, stepping through the door of my studio apartment as though I had stepped from one dream into another.

What I remember was the *heat.*

It began subtly, just a tickle of warmth in my belly. But over time it blossomed and spread until there was a furnace roaring inside me, throwing off waves of heat like it would explode from within me. You could call it a fever—but this was no sickness. Fevers don't talk to you. They don't whisper. They don't put tongues of flame down your arms and legs and...*direct* them, like a hand inside a puppet. And the *color* of it... My God, I could see it like spots dancing in my eyes, clear as anything. Red, red like there was never red before. You can't mix that kind of red with paint, not that I would try. It was like the inside of the sun. The fire inside the fire. I can see it now when I close my eyes tight enough.

But I still didn't really understand what had been done to me. I was still in a deep daze, pacified, an animal drugged for transport. I only stirred when I was home and setting up my easel. I took the brown paper off the canvas and set it on the wood frame. Mechanically, I got my paints from their trunk and poured out a lot of white onto a paper plate. I began to come out of it. When I put the brush down in the white, staring up at that half-complete portrait on the canvas, I realized what I was about to do. But I couldn't stop myself. How can you struggle when there's nothing to struggle against? There was nothing to get my hands around, nothing to brace against. I wasn't even watching from outside myself. It was like I simply wasn't there at all.

In long, straight strokes, I painted the whole canvas white, three coats. I painted right over that lovely, lovely portrait. I'd spent a week creating it, dammit. A week of sketching and planning and painting, and now it's gone. Hell, maybe it was four coats of white paint. I stopped counting after the first. I was sobbing on the inside. I couldn't really cry, you understand. He wouldn't let me—because he didn't feel anything for my past work. He didn't care what we were destroying. I doubt he even thought about it.

That's when I realized what he'd done. This is the part I don't think you'll believe. That freshman kid, he'd...got hold of me somehow. Hollowed me out, pushed me aside to step into my skin, one arm at a time, like putting on a coat. And that red flame I felt, I *saw*, behind my eyelids—*that was him*. The real him. I don't know what that thing in the Dublin Building hall was, the flesh-thing that looked like a boy but wasn't. Maybe it didn't exist. A projection, or a disguise. Maybe he grew it, like a snail grows its shell, slowly over time. A temporary home until something new, something better, came slithering along. Something like *me*.

That's how the three-day horror began.

I did not paint at first. The white on the canvas was not dry, and even the creature roosting in my bones knew better than to work on top of that. Instead, from some far-flung corner of my consciousness, an image began forming. A face was taking shape, floating up as though from beneath thick slime. A girl's face, with thin brown hair framing pale slender features. Small dark eyes under thin brows, a trim nose, a small and almost lipless mouth. I don't remember what she wore, for my gaze never dropped past her chin. But I could imagine the rumpled hoodie, orange and black with the Armistice College jack-o'-lantern on the stomach. *It was her*, Marshall. Sure as I'm sitting here. It was, and could only be, her.

And yet, how can I be sure at all? All this I beheld for only a fraction of a moment before her face began to *change*. And had I any feeling left in my body, I would have been stricken to the ground with horror. Yes, the face was changing; at first, it was as though she was becoming transparent, layer by layer. I could peer through her skin, see the structure of the delicate muscles that controlled her expressions, thin enough to snap under the protective dermis, stretched across the pale skull. I could see the blood pulsing through them, squeezing between the meat and the bone. Then even these muscles were torn loose and only the skull remained, plates of bone meeting as neatly as bricks in a wall. Then this too vanished, and I beheld the brain-superstructure, then the gray jelly quivering within, and beyond that...

The brain is not the center of the skull. There are layers within, and layers within those layers. I've seen them...the faces within the face. I won't lie to you and say there aren't words to describe it. There are. I've whispered them to myself in blind fugue ever since I escaped that place. What I saw was the gleam of eyes from within a hollow tree. The flicker of a candle in the gaping mouth of a carved pumpkin. The furtive movements of something hidden. Something concealed. Something that squirmed in flesh like a maggot. Waiting. Growing. *Feasting.*

You just have to see her like I see her. But I still didn't understand. Not yet. Not quite.

I finally began to paint—and it was like no painting I'd ever rendered before. I hardly looked at the canvas at all. That thing...that gleaming, scurrying *thing*...it burned before my eyes like a flame dancing on the head of a match. I don't remember what marks I made on the canvas, what colors I mixed—indeed, no earthly colors could have hoped to capture the awesome visage that blazed like the face of Hell within me. But stroke by methodical stroke, *something* was taking its shape on my easel. I could not see my own work, but after two hours of toil I began to *feel* it, radiating a strange heat, a terrible power to match the power that held me in its grip. But it was not complete. It was not the real likeness *he* wanted.

I can still smell the stink of that room, Marshall. I've showered, but I can still call up that death-stink, the stench of piss and shit. Remember—I said three days. But like so many other things, I cannot say for sure that was the exact time I spent trapped in the cage of my own body, a slave to the red heat that boiled my blood and commanded my flesh. At first my captor was fairly gentle. Every so often I was allowed to stop working and rest my arms. I could feed myself, or rather, be fed. And of course, I was dispatched to the restroom to relieve myself. But it wasn't long before this small mercy waned. He was frustrated by my lack of progress. I worked into the night, my eyes dry and burning, my eyelids feeling like they were held up by tiny hooks, and when next I felt a stirring in my bowels...

Well, I won't describe that. Not in detail, not to you. But I can see on your face that you're imagining it. Maybe you can even feel the shame I felt, the disgust. No matter. Even this I grew numb to. Hours crawled by, or perhaps they flew. I limped along in a half-dream, my lips dry, my eyes half-closed. But my right hand that gripped the paintbrush held forever steady—because *he* willed it. I don't know if he ever allowed me to sleep. But I must have continued eating and drinking—the evidence is plain enough on the floor of my apartment and smeared on my old clothes. But I could no longer feel the needs that drove those things. Hunger, fatigue... I couldn't feel his moods swirling in me either. Even when twice his frustration overwhelmed him and he raised my fists to tear through the canvas, I felt nothing, only some dim recognition that I'd picked up my arms. I drifted. I ceased to exist. Maybe I'd never existed at all...

Ø

And then it was over. Or only beginning. My mind—it's scrambling and re-scrambling, trying to calm the waters... Like a hand going slack inside a glove, I felt the hold loosen. The scales fell away from my eyes. I was still in my apartment. I didn't know how much time had passed. I felt stifled, smothered, as though I was wrapped in gauze. I blinked in a strange half-light. Dawn? Dusk? I stood slowly, trying to orient myself, shaking the last flecks of red from my vision. My body was stiff all over, and I could not distinguish the pain of one component of my body from that of another. I felt like a rusty door hinge, stiff and crusted. The stink of excrement filled the air; my clothes cleaved to my skin, a vile sensation. I wept briefly and violently, then stopped as suddenly as I'd begun.

The painting was gone.

Yes, *gone*. The easel still stood on the table, and next to it lay my palette, the paints river-bottom dry in their wells. But that portrait—if it was a portrait at all—had vanished. I might as well come out and say it: That terrible masterwork I slaved over, bled over, for three days on end...I never saw it finished. Even if I wanted to describe it, I could not. But I'm grateful, yes, *grateful* for that mercy. Maybe it was a masterpiece as I've described. I don't care. It's out there now, in the world. I won't look for it—the reason why will be clear soon enough.

I showered, naturally. It seemed to take forever to scrape the filth off myself. I got under the water in all my clothes, squeezing my eyes shut against the abominable sensation of my own leavings loosening and crumbling off me into the drain. Then I stripped, and scrubbed and scrubbed. The stench refused to leave my nostrils. God, I scrubbed myself raw. I'm red all over even now, under these clothes. I stayed until the hot water ran out, and a few more minutes after that, then climbed out and fished for a towel. I stood there, drying my face in front of the mirror, for several moments. And when I looked up—

I thought I would be too worn down to scream. But no, the sound came rasping out of me, like hot musty air through old ducts. At first I could only groan, but then—a torrent! A gusher, a geyser of a cry! I raised my hands to my cheeks, then quickly thrust them down to my sides again. I didn't want to touch what I saw in the glass. Can you imagine looking at another human face as though you'd never seen one before? Seeing pink flesh—and *recoiling* at how it felt, *how it must feel*, when it wriggles and crawls under your touch? Studying the planes of a face as though they are the landscape of some hostile planet, orbiting a faraway alien star? To look into somebody else's eyes and see *nothing*...no soul, no intellect...no light at all, save for what reflects off the sclera? That's what leered back at me from my bathroom mirror, real and solid as anything. I braved a touch. I felt flesh under my fingers. Again, I felt the urge to scream—but I could not tear my eyes away, because horror of horrors, *it was still my face!* That was the monstrous thing. I could recognize every feature, every wrinkle...but I couldn't look myself in the eye for more than an instant without feeling bile rise in my throat.

I don't know how *he* stood it. Seeing us, all of us, just like that every moment of every day. Surrounded by us. Alone in a world packed to bursting with twisted parodies of life, with such gormless, slack-faced monsters... I've got a beating heart still. I can feel for him—even after everything. I can imagine his disgust. And I can conjure his hatred too, the hatred that must fester in his own heart. Hate for us, for humans. For the snuffed candles, the hollow trees that grew, dead and swaying, in his world. For *flesh*. For anything not-him, him and his faceless bride. The brutal dichotomy of it! The cosmic solitude!

And yes—I do mean *all of us*. I asked you to turn the mirror away, and now you know why. But perhaps you've noticed I won't meet your eye either. I'm sorry. But politeness doesn't matter anymore. I've had my steering moment...and whatever lever he threw inside of me can't be un-thrown. I'm sick inside now, sick and rotting. There's desperation clawing within me, verging on some brutal, whirlwind frenzy... I had to leave my apartment, you see, to come here. I had to go out and walk among the other students. I dressed myself first, then fired off an email to my arts professor and set about to the grisly business of disposing of my paints and brushes. I felt nothing as I did this. I left and came here, to campus. It was only early evening, and there were still plenty of other students coming down the center walk. I must have been some spectacle, staggering crazily down the sidewalk beside them, every muscle rebelling. They stared, naturally, and I stared back. For the first time in my life, I could not stop staring.

They all had the same face, Marshall. The blank face. The lightless face. *My* face.

There's the real terror! There's the real truth! I had thought that surely the slack-faced horror in the mirror was only a personal affliction, that my encounter with the master of the hollow trees had scooped me out, burned me empty. But no: I could look through each face I beheld in that teeming crowd, passing under the cold bright lamps on the center walk. If I stared long enough, I could peel back the layers of flesh with my eyes. Muscle, bone, brain...and at their center, nothing. They were all empty. Empty like *me*.

Suddenly I was running. Even though I had no strength left in my body, I took off in a dead sprint, their pale slack faces whipping by like the taillights of cars, all staring, staring. I made it almost the whole way here, only stopping just outside the double doors of the Manor to catch my breath. God—my lungs burned, but worse was the horrible awareness that came with it. I was conscious of the construction of my body in a way that filled me up with revulsion. I could imagine the muscular action of my diaphragm, the cavity of my chest filling with air, the vascular pump of my heart, the squirt of blood through the tubes of my veins... I felt the urge, the overpowering thrust, to *destroy* this body, to rid myself of the appendage, the parasite of my own flesh. My fingers raked my face, stretched the skin, nearly drew blood...

But the feeling passed as quickly as it had come. I was here, just at your doorstep. I was careful not to catch sight of myself in the glass doors, but I knew instinctively that if I could get inside, if I could see you, *talk to you*, I could face all the rest of it. But that's not how it happened. I hadn't realized I wasn't alone on the patio. There was another student, a girl, sitting on the bench with one leg crossed over the other and her hands stuffed in the pockets of an orange-and-black sweatshirt. I froze; she blew a long stream of cold-weather fog and half-turned toward me, her face in shadow from the bushes at her back.

"I know you, don't I?" she said—but there was no question in her thin voice. She knew who I was, just as I knew her. She leaned forward, her hair tumbling across her face as she made to stand. Her face swam into view under the streetlamp... I don't need my finished portrait now. I've met my model. His muse. His bride. His *mate*. I've seen the true likeness in the flesh, or something beyond flesh. I've looked it in the face, seen the eyes behind the eyes blinking in the cold lights of our world. The mirror was nothing. The students on the center walk were nothing. This was only madness. Screaming bedlam, veiled in a too-thin human mask. And yet...

And yet I wasn't *afraid* somehow, Marshall. In fact, I felt all fear melt from me like snow sliding off a steep roof. She stood and spoke to me in a quiet voice that might have been pleasant if it hadn't come from that face, from those same lipless lips I'd painted. And I felt something take hold of me. Not him, no, I never felt his white-hot grip again. This was a different power. Something newer, something sweeter. I embraced it eagerly, clung to it like a drowning man clings to driftwood. I finally understood. I could look through her flesh as well, and here, *here* was the real thing at last. Here was the flickering candle in the dark window. I can't find it in your face or even in my own eyes—but there it was, gleaming under this strange girl's skin, gleaming and lively and *true*. Truer than flesh. Truer than anything. I don't need to tell you she was beautiful. Among the shambling slack horrors, she was light—light all the way down.

She grinned almost shyly at me, kicking the back of one sneaker with the toe of the other. "I liked your portrait," she began. "I liked it very much. I don't know how I'll ever be able to thank you. Only..."

I blew through those double doors into your building like Hell itself was scrabbling behind me. Maybe you heard me coming. You certainly would have as I came up the stairs. You'll remember how I pounded your door, how I begged to be let inside, crying out in the hall. How I collapsed, here on this couch, unable to breath or speak or look at you dead-on. But I was not afraid for my life. I didn't need your protection or anyone else's.

All I need is the courage to finish what I started.

He said I needed to see her the way he saw her. Now I do. *And I cannot refuse her.*

"I was wondering," she began again cautiously, "if I could ask you for one more favor. I was wondering—would you be willing to paint one of *him* as well?"

So, thanks for the alcohol. It's steadied me enough. No, don't get up. I can find the door fine. I've got work to do, and my commissioners reward efficiency. Oh, my paints? Yes, all destroyed, like I told you. And my promise to never hold a brush again stands. *But there are other ways to render a real likeness.* Better ways, and better canvases on which to render them. You'll see soon enough. You won't see *me*, of course, but don't be afraid. I'm not frightened at all. I've had my steering moment. I saw the fork coming, and I took it.

And I *can* see the other path, Marshall. I can see you on the shore, beckoning, beckoning.

Oh yes, I can see you. But I'm not jumping back.

...but stroke by methodical stroke, something was taking shape on my easel.

Copilot

I shut my eyes and I'm on the planet's surface again.

I shut my eyes and all that road noise dwindles down to a rumble, and then to nothing. My Jeep Grand Cherokee fades to shadow. The steering wheel goes misty in my hands. I'm tucked up snug in my somma-pod for the lunar cycle, hanging by my hind-limbs in a state of trance.

My name's Grover Tattle. I'm thirty-four years old. Ex-Air Force. Twenty-Third Airborne. Honorable discharge, no decorations. From outside I look like any other man my age. Flesh and blood, with skin and teeth and chest hair and whatever else goes in between. Shake my hand, you'll feel flesh gripping yours. You'll know with a hundred percent certainty I'm a man just like you. But when I close my eyes I can feel Mother-Teacher stroking my mantle soothingly, singing the moonsong in her high lutish voice.

I can't give you details you don't already know. At least: I can't tell you much. You know about the war already, Doctor. You've read your history texts, or at least you followed the news. The fact was this: Our side wasn't going to win it. Even with all our great big bombs and planes and Tomahawk missiles, we didn't have a meatball's chance. There's the genius of the enemy program. They out-bred us. They would take us like an anthill takes a termite mound. Superior numbers. The fight was over hundreds of years before it began. That's the calculus. But we still found a way somehow—didn't we?

You know about the Cubes too. The Cubes turned the tide. The enemy had the numbers. They had the manpower. But we had the Cubes—and against the Cubes their swarm tactics didn't mean a damned thing. Five years ago in March, our CO marched us down to the hangar for a briefing; in the middle of the big concrete floor there were these five big vehicles covered up by tarps held in place by thick ropes and bungee cords all over. Next to these stood two men. One was short with a red face like a steak, and the other was a head taller and wore thick gleaming glasses. Both of them were wearing expensive black suits and decorated like generals, but for some reason they didn't look military to me. I saw the other guys saluting so I saluted too.

Our CO introduced the men in the dark expensive suits as Doctors So and So, and right away they took command of the briefing. The short man with the red steak face did all the talking. He said a lot of long, impressive words about the Enemy and Our Country and how we were all Fighting the Good Fight Together, lots of the kinds of things people who haven't been in the shit like to say to soldiers to make themselves feel important.

Then the tall man with the thick glasses started to pull the tarp off one of the big somethings in the room—and then there it was in the room with us, huge and gleaming under the big LED hangar lights. It looked a bit like one of those old kids' toys. A Rubik's Cube. Of course this wasn't the real article. The real Cubes were three stories tall and wouldn't have crammed into even our biggest hangar. What they showed us was a model. But we got the idea. We all nodded our heads and mooched out our lips appreciatively. Then our CO stepped forward and said:

"We need ten big strong men to fly this spacecraft."

Strong men, he said. That's important, I think, Doctor. Not brave men. Not smart men. Brains don't enter into it at all. Flying a Cube's all muscle, it turns out. But we didn't understand it all at the time. What we knew is that our commanding officer had just asked us for ten big strong men. That day, nine of the biggest sumbitches I ever saw took one proud step forward. And me, being one of the biggest and the strongest, I stepped forward too.

You ever seen a Q-Bert for real, Doctor? Not many pictures of them ever got on the news, I don't think. Most you've seen are fakes—photoshopped, or artist renditions. But a few of the real deal came across independent channels every so often. Those got taken down the fastest by Big Brother Sam, of course. But I saw one once, a real one, as close to me as I am to you now. Big sumbitch, a Q-Bert is. That's how they fly those big spacecraft they've got all by themselves, with all those fiddly moving parts on the insides. Bigger than ten men, all heads and legs, like a big octopus. With a funny tube-mouth just like a tube of lipstick, but with teeth in rings going all down into the gullet. They've got a proper name, I think, but after those first drawings got loose in the world everybody started calling them Q-Berts on account of those snouts.

The first and last time I ever saw one, I was under sedation and just about to go under. They were wheeling us into the operating theater, one after the other in a line like train cars. They had us on flat gurneys with our faces pointed up at that piercing white ceiling. I was the last man they brought in. My wingman, Jools, went in before me, but he got a heavier dose of the dope and was out cold when they pushed him through the curtain. My turn came, and Doctors So and So came out and asked me how I was feeling. Then the short red-faced one started in on his God and Country speech again and I started thinking about baseball.

Two orderlies came around behind me and pushed me through into a small white room with a very bright light overhead. They left me there, drifting on the edge of consciousness from the dope, while they prepared their instruments. Up on the second level, I saw a ring of faces. There was my commanding officer, as well as maybe a half-dozen older gray men with gray suits and lined gray faces. I tried to smile at them, but my face was numb and didn't want to smile. The gray men turned away from me and began talking in low voices to each other, so I turned away too and tried to look around the room I was in.

I craned my neck to the left, then to the right—and realized we weren't alone in the operating theater. On a raised platform only a few feet from my head lay a strange creature, tied down with thick straps and lying motionless. Of course it was a Q-Bert. I'd heard the rumors a few times, of something crash-landed in a Texas desert somewhere, something big as a house with more legs than you could count on your fingers. The thing lay still, and its funny tube mouth drooped off the edge of the platform, hanging limp. One huge Frisbee eye stood open but glassy, sort of smoothed over like a glass eye in a doll's face. The Q-Bert was dead or doped like I was, but for some reason I felt like that one massive eye was looking at me, looking through me, asking me for something. A heard a rustle of fabric to my left—and suddenly the eye snapped shut.

I was so rattled I didn't think to wonder why the doctors were strapping me down as well.

Here's the part of the story where I'm supposed to say, "...and I don't remember too much after that." But it's not true. I remember enough. They didn't dope me all the way. I was awake when they opened me up. Foggy, sure, and numb as a fence post, but conscious. That's important, Doctor—every so often I'll get flashes, little micro-pictures from that operating theater. They shaved my head and waxed it, then they took a one-inch square off the top of my skull. I remember faces leaning over, looking down into that hole, breathing through surgical masks.

Then somebody said: "Now we're all sons of bitches."

I remember his shadow crossing my face. Then they stuck a needle through the hole in my head and filled my skull up with pain and blinding light.

How do you teach a man to fly an alien spacecraft? That was the trick. Even once they got the Cubes operational, nobody knew how to fly them. I flew an F-11 for the Twenty-Third Airborne. I couldn't tell you how to do it. When you're flying something that big and that loud and that fast, your brain's got no part in it. Your hands and feet know how to fly, what switches to flip or what pedals to depress to get you out of a screaming nosedive a hundred feet above the ocean. You can't teach that. You've got to learn it yourself. The memories live in your bones and your muscles, in your eyes and ears and joints.

I felt the big needle go in, despite the dope. Whoever's hand it was trembled a little as he pushed the plunger. I could feel cold steel noodling around in my brain tissue. Hurt like a bastard. I think I screamed, but in that strange moment I couldn't be sure it wasn't the creature beside me who'd cried out instead. I remember there was a big commotion to my immediate right. From the corner of my eye I saw long fleshy structures waving above me, bending several times at joints like elbows. The screaming filled the room up. The arms, waxy and many-jointed, tossed surgical equipment and knocked aside the big light above us. The doctors left my side—in an instant the pain in my head spiked like a blast of hot white starlight and I *tore through my restraints* like a wild animal, roaring and screaming and flailing—then, I woke up a while later on my cot at the airbase with a slight headache but feeling overall completely fine.

I'll ask again: How do you teach a man to fly an alien spacecraft? You make him remember how to fly. Alien recall in his blood, alien thoughts in his skull. You steal him the memories he needs from some far-flung star, and as long as he's a big strong sumbitch who's used to obeying orders, he'll do the job and he won't ask you why. We flew that Cube, us ten big strong men. Only we weren't ten men any longer. They made us one creature, those doctors. One unit, one machine, one whole sumbitch like they'd stitched us together at the foreheads. We all got memories from the same Q-Bert, you understand. That's why they needed ten—one for each arm. I told you how big those bastards are.

Here's a disappointing fact for you. I don't remember the Battle of Lhodad at all. I could give you the official spin they gave the papers, but you've read that all already. Anyhow, it was five years ago. Where I was in the Cube didn't even have a window. I was stuck down in a metal hole in a wall with my arms wrapped around a joystick, working one of six thrusters. I couldn't see a thing going on outside. But I could feel it. All of us could feel it—alien rage, star-crushing frustration, bloodlust hot enough to dim a sun. Only Jools, my wingman, and Old Yarnell got window seats on that flight of ours. Only they saw how many men we killed that day. They were working the turrets hanging from the Cube's bright smooth belly.

They say now that it was a lot of people who died at Lhodad. We never found out how many, not even a ballpark sum. I think they kept that information from us on purpose, for fear of... Well, for fear of what? I've wondered that for a long time.

Then the war was all won—and they let us go. Honorable discharges all around. The message was obvious though: Don't come back. You could see it in the faces of the brass, even when they were pinning medals on our chests and clapping us on the back. The fear, the suspicion. The unease. None of them would look us in the eye. Nobody knew what they'd made us. None of us ever saw Doctors So and So again. So we went home and started our lives over. We got set up with jobs and families. Wives, husbands, children. We tried to act like everything was normal, that nothing had happened to us. I tried real hard for a real long time.

For a while, I thought it might be working.

Then—at first, we didn't understand what was happening to us. There was something inside all of our heads. A flicker, a small burst of emotion, quivering against the huge opaque stranger of our consciousness. Then there was the name. *Quazl*. The realization chimed in all our heads at once, like a gong. It was the exact moment when you're screwing in a lightbulb and the light comes on for the first time. Instantaneous contact. The Q-Bert on the table in the operating theater, she'd had a name. She'd had a life. A life we could all suddenly remember in hard shocking detail. And that's when it all came flooding back in. The rage, the bloodlust, the fear and denial and hard cold despair. They'd given us everything, those doctors. They couldn't see the rim of the mug; they hadn't known, couldn't have known, when to stop pouring.

Old Yarnell was the first to go. His twin grandsons found him in the barn, swinging from a sturdy beam, eyes bugging out of his head like fat white grapes. No note, no will, no warning at all. The reports called it shellshock, but the rest of us, we found out and we knew what had happened to him. But there was nothing we could have done. After that, we began dropping off fairly quickly. Harley, Gavin, Big Boy, Johns—all in about two weeks, maybe a little longer. Jools held out the longest of all of us. They found him down in an old bomb bunker with the back of his head taken off by a hunting rifle. He'd squeezed the trigger with his toes.

Now you know why I'm here. I don't want to be. No offense to you, Doctor, but I don't trust you any further than I can throw you. I've had enough of doctors, white coats or no. But I had to come. Jools was the toughest sumbitch I ever met, and he didn't last two weeks after Quazl woke up. I can feel it inside me, the countdown, the time bomb set to some secret counter, set to implode my brain, make me eat my own gun like Jools did before. I didn't have a family to come back to, and sometimes I wonder if that helped me survive. I didn't have anything to return to that didn't juke with Quazl's fantasy.

You've got to understand: She knows she's dead. She understands perfectly that her body is rotting on a slab in an air force laboratory somewhere in the desert. But when I shut my eyes, I can see a fresh new cocoon woven from gossamer threads anchored to an edifice in Mother-Teacher's housing pod. I can hear Father-Guardian in the next hollow over, humming some phrase of the moonsong in counterpart to Mother-Teacher's sweet vibrating voice. I can smell sunset in the air, feel a hot wind starting to sweep the dust off a new day. You could shake my hand and you'll know with a hundred percent certainty that I'm a man just like you—but when my eyes are closed I stride like a giant across worlds more familiar than my own, circling in decaying orbits the fading light of a distant gleaming star.

There was one more death at Lhodad. Grover Tattle, thirty-four. Ex-Air Force. Ex-anything. I'm sorry, Jools, but I can't hold the line any longer. Quazl's been asking about you, asking to go home. She wants me to take her there in my big strong arms.

I'm running out of ways to tell her no.

Red Meat

Liberty Eppes was afraid.

The first twenty-nine floors of the Malcolm Building were dark, but the top floor—the penthouse—was lit up bright yellow all around, forming a sort of halo atop the lean, almost phallic structure of the high rise. Far below, the streets were clogged with traffic; the angry sound of car horns and brake pedals rose up from the road like the swells of a distant symphony.

But the noise did not reach Liberty, standing at the window of her penthouse, looking down with her forehead pressed against the bulletproof glass. She was in her kimono—the new one, with the red lilies around the hem and down the sleeves—and when she moved, the silk swished against her thighs comfortingly. The wine glass in her left hand was half-emptied, and her fist was white-knuckle tight around the stem.

Liberty tried to remember a time when the glass had made her feel safe. She knew it was a necessary measure—even after all these years, the nature of her work painted a crosshairs on her forehead—but the last time she'd stood in this position and pressed her palm to the smooth flat surface and drawn any security from it was a distant memory. She stepped away from the window, her gaze straying to the display cabinet in the nook across the room. At one time, the shelves had been crammed full—college athletic trophies, altruism awards, framed photographs of her shaking hands with seven consecutive U.S. presidents—but Liberty had grown disgusted with such ornaments and had them packed off somewhere.

Now only one prize remained: on the top shelf, half-hidden in shadow, stood a glass jar containing a human fetus, floating head-down in three gallons of preservative fluid. There was a part of Liberty, a very small part, that felt strange keeping such a grisly trophy from her work, but this jar lent her more courage and will than three inches of bulletproof glass ever could. Here at last was something solid in her world. Here was something she could control.

She gazed into the eyes of the fetus—dark, inky blue through the partially formed eyelids. Like a pen run through the wash, she thought. Like a stain on the crotch of your good jeans. A stain that won't come out no matter how you scrub.

The high growl of the elevator opening startled her, and she whirled around, clutching her kimono shut at her chest. Janet Freiling, who worked in legislative affairs, stepped through the steel double doors, holding a tall, thin gift bag with pink ruffles around the opening in one hand. "I didn't mean to surprise you," she said, shifting her weight from one foot to the other in her white two-inch heels.

"I thought everyone was gone for the night downstairs," Liberty said, recovering quickly.

"Everybody but me," Janet replied. "I had to get some files off my computer." She was wearing the Scala dress again, the white one with the black bar across her chest. It reminded Liberty of a censor bar.

"You're not working tonight, are you?" Liberty asked uneasily. "You've been going hard all week. Take the night off. Have fun."

Janet shook her head. "Can't do it. My team's meeting up with the Sec-East Commission tomorrow afternoon to discuss redistricting, and I've got a dozen more reports to go through before I'm ready to face them. I think they'll swing our way, but I want to be one hundred percent certain." She paused, peering absently down into the open gift bag in her hands. "And plus, I didn't make reservations anywhere," she said sheepishly.

Liberty shrugged. "Youth is wasted on the young. When you get to my age, you'll wish you'd fucked off from work every once in a while." The hand holding her kimono closed shook, but she willed it still with a burst of concentration.

Janet giggled, showing white, brace-straightened teeth. "You're not that old, Ms. E." She thrust the bag forward, dangling it from her fist by its twine handles. "Here," she said. "It's just a little something. From all of us downstairs."

"Will you set it on the counter there?" Liberty said, motioning to the black marble countertop. "Yes, right there's fine. Thank you, Janet." The bag clunked heavily against the marble. Something fragile, Liberty thought. A vase, maybe? "You can go now," she said. "I don't mean to be brusque, but I'd like to be alone right now."

Janet nodded. "Of course." She returned to the elevator, which whined shut behind her. Liberty watched the red digital display tick down: Twenty-five, twenty-four, twenty-three... An image flashed in her mind: the elevator cable snapping, the steel box—with Janet inside—plunging toward the earth, the red light-up numbers accelerating their countdown, racing closer and closer to zero until...

Liberty squeezed her eyes shut, her heart slapping her ribs. No. She needed to be strong tonight. She drained her glass and headed to the cabinet for a refill, feeling the warmth of the alcohol spread down her slim frame. As she poured her wine, she stared at the moon-like face of the grandfather clock in the corner, the angle of its hands tapering toward the zero hour.

When the hour struck, she raised the glass to her lips, and immediately began to cough as the sharp taste of blood filled her mouth. Still coughing, she walked quickly to the sink and poured the blood—for indeed, it was blood now, after all—down the InSinkErator. She poured out what remained of the wine in the bottle as well and deposited the empty in the sink, but kept the glass, holding it down at her side like a hidden dagger. Drops of blood slipped from the rim of the glass and sank into the hem of Liberty's kimono, as well as the white shag carpet beneath her bare feet. She froze, every muscle tensed, listening, waiting for what she already knew was coming.

Tonight was Liberty Eppes' one hundred and fifteenth birthday.

There came a shuffling sound off to her left, low and quiet. Liberty turned toward the source of the noise, feeling the muscles in her neck and chest tighten. Yes, there it was...tiny footsteps approaching from just out of sight. The temperature in the room seemed to surge ten degrees, and her breath roiled hot in her lungs.

Then she saw it: from behind her chair in the sitting room appeared a blobbish, misshapen mass of flesh, tottering on pale, naked legs and struggling to keep its bulbous and veiny head upright. The creature's skin was pale and dull and covered in a thick layer of tacky mucus that squelched when it walked, and its ribs, sharp and thin and innumerable, poked through its jutting, birdlike chest. The severed umbilical cord dragged on behind it like a tail, blood and fluid leaking from the jaggy, fraying end, and the tiny nub of its penis—of course it was a boy, yes, it was always a boy—clung to the inside of one milky thigh.

The creature wobbled forward on its spindly legs, its blue, inkspot eyes sightless behind the pink film of their lids, but when it came within ten feet of Liberty its head snapped toward her, quick and sudden like the movement of a marionette. Then it opened its wet pink hole of a mouth and emitted a sound, a thin, reedy cry...a keening sound, high and hungry like a baby bird calling. Like the scream of a police siren approaching. The noise sent bolts of terror punching into Liberty's gut, and she reacted with a spasmodic motion of her arm: the wine glass shattered *krishhh* against the marble countertop, and she brandished the jagged edge at the tottering, mewling form, her whole arm trembling violently with anticipation. The creature staggered closer, its high, raking cry rising to its ear-shattering climax. Liberty resisted the urge to pray.

"Come on, then!" she finally screamed. The monster lunged for her throat.

And then it was upon her, sending her toppling over backward, her kimono flying open, her fist still clutching the stem of the broken wine glass as she fell, shrieking, to the floor. They rolled together on the shag carpet: Liberty felt its skin sliding across hers, its mucus adhering to her clothes, its doll-like hands pawing at her bare breasts. She felt panic oozing up her throat, and she tried to swallow it, imprison it inside her, but the monster was strong...too strong to be so small, strong and it was *winning*. Its weight crushed into her chest, its tiny fists beat at her face, the slimy length of the umbilical cord found its way around her neck and started tightening...

And then her fist tightened around the stem of the wine glass and she plunged the jagged edge into the thrashing form on top of her. Hot blood squirted up her arm and the monster let out a scream of pain, but Liberty pulled the glass out and stabbed downward again and again, *chulk-chulk-chulk*, feeling the sharp point sinking into the soft flesh over and over and over.

Then it was over. The quivering mass of flesh lying across her heaving chest stopped quivering and hung limp, its bulging cranium rolling face-down in a pool of blood on the carpet. *It was stronger this year*. The thought flickered like heat lightning in Liberty's mind. It was stronger this year. It would never stop getting stronger.

She shook herself and stood up, shoving the corpse to one side. She took four quick strides to the kitchen and pulled open a drawer and rooted through it until she found what she was looking for: a steak knife, the one with the wooden handle. Then she returned to the mess on the floor and without hesitating plunged the knife into the creature's shoulder, slicing and cutting until she tore out a chunk of meat and fat, which she then shoved into her mouth. She chewed the meat quickly, ignoring the juice dribbling down her chin, then swallowed. Already her hands were working again, sawing off another hunk of meat from the blobby shoulder muscle.

Liberty kept eating, there on the floor, her hand slimy around the knife, until the grandfather clock struck one and she decided she could hold no more. She staggered to her feet, meat-drunk and heavy, leaning against the counter for support. Her head swam; her abdomen felt bloated and stiff. She could feel the process beginning already: all across her body there came a distinct shrinking sensation, as though she were being squeezed through a rubber tube just slightly narrower than herself. The skin on her face lifted and tightened; the quivering flaps under her arms shrank away; the dark blue veins around her ankles faded into her flesh. The years slid off her body as smoothly as dropping a towel to the floor, and Liberty breathed a sigh of relief, a breath that smelt faintly of time and blood.

Only then did she reach for the gift bag on the countertop. In one quick motion of her hand she tore open the staples holding the bag shut and the white tissue paper underneath, revealing the cork and long glass neck of a wine bottle concealed beneath—*Marcello Rosso*, 1947. Tied to the neck with red ribbon was a small note written in Janet's pretty looping handwriting on a little card. Liberty smiled a crimson dribbling smile as she read:

From us to you –

A reminder that if you aren't at the table then you're on the menu –

Tastes best paired with red meat.

Last Supper

Corpumond reached for his fork. The purple sun hung low in that angry blistered sky, its bloodshot eye scrutinizing the scorched earth below. The last Big Bomb dropped over two months before, but that stink lingered, that last vague trace of ozone and radiation that seared the nostrils like mustard gas. Corpumond and his wife sat on the roof of what had been the Caffur-Morris building, the tallest freestanding structure not knocked down at the knees by the Big Bombs. The streets below them were barren save for a hot breeze whisking gray ash around the sidewalks in little circles. Small fires blazed like television sets in the windows of the empty skeletons of buildings.

Reaching the fork was no small task. Corpumond's tremendous belly ballooned his waistband like wind pushing out a sail, pressing taut against the table's edge. Reaching anything on the table required Corpumond to rise up in his chair, struggling both against the wood digging into his flesh and against his own substantial gravity. But Corpumond was proud of his stomach. Nearing the end, after the last Bombs fell, he'd seen people on the street withering down to nothing from hunger: emaciated, hollow-eyed husks stalking the alleyways. Not Corpumond. He and his wife could eat anything, and stayed fat. Corpumond used to pity the husks—pity them, and resent them. There was no meat on their bones, so they were useless to him and Ellisanae.

Across the big table, Ellisanae cleared her throat. "Wotta swell spread," she said for the third time in ten minutes.

The table between them was eleven by six feet and heaped with platter after platter of foodstuffs, the finest post-Big Bomb cuisine available. Mostly sea life—the Bombs left the oceans largely untouched—along with hardier critters and flora lining the edges of the banquet like parsley.

Dolphin. Crabgrass. Pumpkin. Penguin. Brain coral. Boll weevil. Kudzu. Kelp. Crocodile. Catnip. Leather boot. Tortoise. Tire tread. Tuna. Humboldt squid. Sea snake. Blowfish. Beets.

This is the last supper, Corpumond thought. The last feast in the world.

"Wotta swell spread," Ellisanae repeated.

Corpumond looked across the table at his wife. Her black eyes squinted out of her puttied face, glinting like marbles pressed into clay. Her skin, like her stomach, was stretched tight around her ruddy face and neck, and her plump breasts sagged to the table, mounds of dough resting on the wood. Ellisanae weighed thirty-two stone, just twenty pounds less than Corpumond himself.

"Tuck in," Corpumond said.

They began eating, descending on their meal like carrion birds thrusting their heads into the open flank of a carcass. They spoke little, and when they did, it was always to ask the other to pass something, some condiment or side dish. The piles of food dwindled rapidly—Corpumond and Ellisanae chewed thoroughly, but took very big bites.

"Coral's a bit tough," mumbled Corpumond through a mouthful.

"Mayonnaise'll soften it right up," said Ellisanae.

"Is there any left?"

"Nope," said Ellisanae, spooning the last of the mayonnaise onto her rump roast. The lump of flesh on her plate was pale pink and bore a Heart Mom tattoo. This was quickly covered by the mayonnaise. "Trade you for some of that dolphin though."

Corpumond shook his head. "I got the blowhole," he replied. "Best part on a dolphin. Tender."

"You always get the blowhole."

Corpumond stuck his tongue out at her and shoveled in another bite of blubber. The texture was rubbery, but oddly porous, like dense sea sponge. Across the table, Ellisanae ripped off a big bite of the last known sea sponge and shoved it into her mouth.

"That about does it for the seafood," she mumbled through a mouthful of sponge.

Corpumond shook his head, sending flecks of salty dolphinflesh flying from his swinging jowls. "I've been saving something real special," he said.

"Oh, treat, you didn't," Ellisanae squealed as Corpumond reached beneath his seat. He produced a covered tray, and when he lifted the lid, seven perfect tubeworms lay stacked neatly beneath, crusty and puckered and glistening red. Ellisanae clapped her hands.

"Filched 'em outta the aquarium a week ago," Corpumond said. "Happy anniversary, pumpkin."

They divided the worms between them, Ellisanae taking the larger share. Corpumond devoured his with knife and fork, eating them two at a time, while Ellisanae ate slowly—contemplatively, almost—using her fingers. She paused, one flaccid tubeworm held between her thumb and forefinger, and smiled. The smile spread her cheeks like dough on a cookie sheet. There was tubeworm juice dribbling from one corner of her lips.

"You know," she said brightly, "I think this is the best anniversary we've had."

"Sorry?" said Corpumond, chewing.

"No, really," said Ellisanae. "I like this. When have we ever eaten so well?" She shoved the tubeworm into her mouth and chewed the crispy carapace slowly, savoring the briny flavor. "I wish they'd drop Bombs every year, just for us."

Corpumond swallowed his last bite of worm and threw down his fork and knife. "Well, that's the end of that," he said, pushing back his chair.

Ellisanae slipped a knife into her sleeve and pushed her chair back as well. She heaved to her feet and dragged her chair across the roof until it was next to Corpumond's and sat down beside him. Corpumond took her hand, and the two looked out at the horizon where the sun was just starting to sink. Ellisanae belched and yawned, and while her eyes were closed Corpumond lifted the big serving fork off the platter with his other hand and held it at his side, out of sight. The metal was cool and oddly comforting against his bare thigh.

"When have we ever eaten so well?" Ellisanae repeated.

Corpumond's heart clamped like a fist, and he gave his wife's hand a squeeze. Ellisanae sighed happily and returned the squeeze. The knife in her sleeve slid to her elbow and stuck there, nestled against the pale, folded skin. The purple, dying sun continued to struggle across the sky, and somebody's stomach growled.

She's New in Town

Paul Bellamy saw the shape of her moving through the double doors of the Quick-E-Mart in the fisheye mirror whose eye looked into all the hidden spaces behind the white metal shelves and stacks of cans and boxes of the little convenience store. She walked in and shook water off her blue raincoat—momentarily blocking his view of the Williams boy reading some trashy magazine off the rack by the door—and started toward the refrigerated section in back. The boy's pimpled face turned and squinted at the girl's backside with some interest, but turned back to his literature once he lost sight of her behind the pastry shelf. Outside, rain continued to pour.

Paul watched her scan the alcohol in the back, trying to guess her age in the fisheye's reflection. She couldn't have been more than seventeen, he wagered in his head, but it was hard to tell at that distance. It happened every week or so: a girl like that coming in, trying to flash a fakey or an older sister's driver's license. Paul had a girl show him her breasts once. He hadn't asked; she just sidled up to the counter, thumped a six-pack next to the register, and pulled up her shirt. He let her off without much lecture. She'd been his neighbor's daughter, and only fifteen years old.

The Williams boy sneezed twice and put the magazine back on the rack before wiping his nose with the back of a hand, then his hand on the seat of his blue jeans. He ambled up to the counter and slid a pack of Marlboros forward. "For my older brother," he said, glancing away.

"Sure," Paul said. Mitch Williams was nineteen and the state of his lungs was his own concern. "You know who she is?" he asked, angling his chin at the girl's reflection.

The Williams boy looked, shook his head. "Nah. Guess she's new."

"Or an out-of-towner." Paul frowned. Usually Mitch could be counted on to know the names of girls—even the new ones. "Six thirty-five for the smokes."

The Williams boy paid and made his exit, pulling his jacket up over his head against the torrent, and Paul went back to watching the girl. She'd lost interest in the alcohol and was now browsing a sunglasses display, rotating the case back and forth and peering at her reflection in the lenses. Pretty soon she plucked a pair of aviators off their hook and trudged up to the register. At this point, Paul got his first real look at her: she was a tall skinny thing, oddly proportioned, all elbows and ankles. She had a pale almost yellowy mask of a face framed by curtains of dark wet hair, with pale pink cheeks and extremely chapped lips that were almost white with dead skin. Her raincoat was far too big for her body; with her arms at her sides, the sleeves hung low enough to cover all but the ends of fingers tipped in shiny black nail polish that was starting to chip. She'd put on the aviators on her way to the register, hiding her eyes.

"Four ninety-nine," Paul told her, squinting at the tag dangling off one side of the glasses. "You'll need to take those off so I can scan them."

The girl frowned and started fiddling with one arm of the sunglasses, but did not remove them. To his surprise, Paul found himself wondering if she'd break for the door. The Quick-E-Mart had been robbed at gunpoint twice in the past three years. Both times, a pair of young men had come in near closing wearing hooded sweatshirts, the drawstrings pulled tight around their faces. One would come and pull him over the counter and sit him on the tile floor, putting the barrel of the gun in his face, while the other cleaned out the register. If there wasn't much cash inside, they'd grab as many twelve-packs as they could stack in their arms and run out, shouting backward for Paul not to follow them.

As soon as they left, Paul would call Jonah Leland down at the police station, who'd come around with another officer and get descriptions of the boys and maybe a mug of coffee if the pot was fresh. Paul never found out if the young men were ever caught. Jonah was always talking about Paul getting something to keep behind the counter, a shotgun maybe, but Paul kept thinking about the second robbery, about how the boy holding the gun looked. There was no expression in his eyes, no emotion at all, just a tired kind of look like he didn't know where he was, even though he was the one holding the gun.

"You take AmEx?" the girl asked in a hollow sort of voice, like she had a throatful of phlegm.

Paul said he did. "Still need to scan those first," he repeated. Again the girl hesitated, but she obeyed, folding the sunglasses before clicking them against the counter. Her eyes were bright and clear and olive-colored.

While Paul scanned the tag, the girl plunged one black-tipped hand into her jeans pocket and fished out a pink metal wallet with a clasp and half-a-dozen plastic cards inside. She slid the Am-Ex card forward on the counter. He swiped it; the little screen on the register flashed double zeroes. "No good," Paul said. "Sorry, Miss..."

She frowned again and handed him another card. "Try this."

Another few cards later, they found one that still had some juice, and Paul rang up the sunglasses, feeling a little relieved as he punched in the numbers. "Come on back anytime," he said, handing the sunglasses back. "Guess you won't need a bag." The girl turned to leave, slipping the aviators over her eyes as she went.

"Wait, Miss," Paul called after her. "I forgot your receipt..."

There was a terrific flash of lightning then, followed by the boom of thunder; an explosion shook the Quick-E-Mart as a transformer outside blew. All at once the lights shut off, plunging Paul and the strange girl into near darkness. Something clattered on the floor, and Paul saw the girl's silhouette swoop down after it, her nails scraping the hard tile as she groped in the dark.

Then—almost as though she sensed Paul watching her, she jerked her head up. Paul felt his breath catch like a fishhook inside him. She had night eyes, like a cat's but brighter, with little white disks gleaming in the dark where her pupils should go. Paul made a small gurgling sound in his throat and did not move.

The lights snapped back on. The girl stood and squinted against the sudden glare. Her eyes were the same olive color as before. She and Paul stared at each other a moment, neither of them moving. There was no sound except for their breathing and the steady drum of the rain. Finally, the girl walked up to the counter and snatched the receipt from Paul's hand, leaving parallel scratches on his palm with her nails when their hands briefly touched.

"Thanks," she said—and she put the sunglasses back on, walked out into the thundering rain, crossed the road, and disappeared.

Paul stood there behind the counter until around closing time, and when night fell he went about the motions of closing down the store like he was made of wood, mechanically locking up the register and switching off the rows of florescent lights one by one. As he stepped out the door, the wet stench of the rain filled his nostrils, thick and strong; that first in-breath made him feel like he was drowning. All around him, there was fog rising up off the pavement, swirling in the harsh glow of the outdoor light and threading between his ankles like a living thing, lithe and serpentine. Paul locked the Quick-E-Mart door and climbed into his car. He started the engine but didn't drive away straight off. He sat with the headlights on, staring out the front windshield. His headlights could not penetrate the mist; the world outside looked damp and strange.

Then suddenly the fog cleared for a moment, and Paul found himself staring at the brick wall behind the Quick-E-Mart. His headlights made two white circles on the red brick, enormous and bright and unblinking. His hand ached suddenly—the hand that the girl had scratched with her long dark fingernails. But now there was no mark there to show. Paul shook himself, switched the headlights off, and drove very slowly all the way to his home.

When It Rains

I'm awake before she knocks. *Tap, ta-ta-tap*, against the glass panel. She was on the high school snare line; rhythm lives in her knuckles, hard-wired. I'm out of bed and on my feet, crossing the bedroom. Now the window's pried open, and she's pouring through, collapsing like she's got no bones inside her. This is how it always starts, but my heart still picks up the beat—like it's one of Lisey's snares, taut under my pajamas. She pries herself off the hardwood, dripping all over. There's not much light to see, but she's beautiful. Any idiot could see she's beautiful. The kind of pretty you buy those glamour magazines to see.

Outside, it's raining. It seems like it's always raining now.

She talks with her eyes mostly. *Glad to see you – This weather's shitty – I love you.* The silence takes out any muddled meanings. She touches my shoulder, grinning; her skin's cold from the rain. I get the towel and when she rubs herself dry, it poofs her hair out all over. I laugh—into my hand, so my parents don't get up. And she laughs too, silently, so hard it shakes her whole slender body. I've missed that smile; it hardly matters that I can't hear the laugh with it.

It's all familiar, comforting. Enough so I forget and start feeling good, start hoping. Maybe it'll be different now. Maybe it'll outlast the rain this time.

Lisey's impatient—she throws the towel down and pushes her mouth against me. We fall back against the foot of the bed. I'm damned all over again, condemned. I think maybe she knows what's coming; it chases her rhythm like greyhounds around the track after the digital rabbit. It's warmer under the blankets, even if she's still damp and slick with mud. We tangle together, pressing close. But my hands never flutter lower than her waist. She only had to stop me once. Even now I understand there are some forbidden places, some barriers we can't trespass. We dance along those electric lines; but in the end, the choice isn't ours.

Maybe you've heard this story before. Maybe you know it already.

Too soon, too soon—powerful energy builds outside like a towering hum. Lisey tenses against me; her hands make fists in my clothes. I'm pressed so close I can feel her rhythm quickening. Not a heartbeat but some even more primal vibration, something that persists. She feels it coming a second before I do...and now through the curtains, I see lightning slash the sky. Then: thunder, like an earthquake, like a small apocalypse. It shakes every window in the house.

I feel her go tight all over. She's so stiff that for a moment I can picture it, actually imagine where she really is. But I don't dwell. She's starting to talk, finally.

"Hi—it's me, silly. I'm only a few minutes out now, you'd better be ready. It's really starting to come down out here. I've got my wipers going full steam, but I can barely see... Oh, there's your street. I see you now, just let me—hold on, there's..."

I press my hand over her mouth; it smothers the screech I know comes next. The first time, she bit me so hard it drew blood. I told my parents I fell, that the scar was an old one. This time she relents to the stifle; now she's shaking against me; now she's crying, sobbing, though her sobs sound like a long even hiss, like a rush of static... No tears come out either.

She talks with her body mostly. *I'm scared – I'm cold – Don't let me go again.*

I hold her so tight I'm afraid she'll break, until the shaking stops. Soon she goes still; maybe she's really asleep. Her chest goes up and down, but there's no peace on her face. I try to stay awake. But cradling Lisey to my chest, eventually my eyes push closed. There's rhythm inside her still. It's the rhythm of the rain, driving down, rocking me, lulling me back into oblivion.

Ø

The next morning's Saturday. Lisey's gone—the clock's red numbers say six. I'm not awake but I haul upright; my bed, my clothes, all muddy from her. The room smells like her, and the rain. The house is still asleep. I one-foot hop, sliding on sweatpants, and I towel up the puddle she left on the hardwood near my bed. Then I creep through the dark house, out the front door. The world is so quiet after a storm. No cars, no birds singing yet. The light is hazy and there's a gauzy white mist curling off the road. I walk maybe ten minutes.

I go to the churchyard. I go to the grave. Maybe you've heard this story before.

A young man out travelling meets a strange woman on the road; as a gentleman in those times, he puts his coat on her shoulders against the bitter cold and wind. They come to a crossroads—a bell chimes, and suddenly the young woman has vanished, taking the man's coat with her.

Later in town, none of the locals know the woman, even when he gives her name; it's only by accident that the youth recovers his lost property. His coat is draped across a headstone in the town graveyard. It bears the name of his ghostly companion.

But Lisey leaves no sign. There's no coat of mine, no borrowed sweatshirt, no scarf. The earth isn't even disturbed. There aren't footprints leaving or coming back. She's here. I'm here too.

My phone in my pants pocket, heavy as lead now. Pull it out, numb fingers moving across the touch screen. Play the voicemail on speakerphone. Her voice. Her last words.

"Hi—it's me, silly. I'm only a few minutes out now, you'd better be ready. It's really starting to come down out here. I've got my wipers going full steam, but I can barely see... Oh, there's your street. I see you now, just let me—hold on, there's..."

A screech of brakes, a harsh roar of twisting metal impact. Then a long thin hiss of static.

I put the phone away; my hands find the top of the gravestone as feeling takes me over, bending me forward, pushing me to earth. The teachers, the kids in the hallway...their stares are a cage. And my house is too quiet; my parents hold their breath, walking on eggshells. But here I can feel Lisey sobbing against me, terrified of the thunder. I can hear her breath quicken because the rain is too hard, coming down too fast to see through, even with the windshield wipers going full blast. I can see her searching for me in the dark, that first night, finding me.

Refusing to move on. Me, refusing to let go. Loving her still.

It won't last. Nothing lasts—not the rain, not Lisey's visits. Not even this lingering eulogy. Soon she'll sleep; I want it for her, desperately. A part of me wants it. But the other part is a dark hole, crumbling at the edges, yawning wider and hungrier in me. That part's scared of the thunder too. One night it'll rain, and she won't come back. I won't even look for her. The rhythm at my window will be tree branches, or a bird's beak, or nothing at all. It makes me a little crazy sometimes, thinking about it, but only a little. I guess it's all I think about now.

The world starts to wake up around me. I hear a car's engine in the distance, the low squeal of tires on wet pavement. My feet start back toward the house. The mist hasn't cleared. The tires are closer; maybe it's on the same street, coming at me, blind as Lisey's driver. I don't look for it. My sneakers dance along the center line of the road, back and forth—to Lisey's rhythm.

My eyes are in the pale sky; I'm looking for rainclouds. It seems like it's always raining now.

Sometimes You Bet Two

The dark was thicker, there out in the country.

Joan Parker shivered against the window glass. Outside her Jeep Wrangler, the night had clotted, bringing out early stars. She and Barb Cobb were parked under the fizzing lights of a Shell station, but across the horse field on the other side of the road the dark was impregnable. Maybe space was the root cause, Joan considered. Wide-open expanses for shadows to grow in. Or maybe there was less light here to chase them away. But the darkness beyond those high yellow lights *was* thicker, laying in drifts across the cold bleak countryside.

Heavy like gravy, Joan decided. Like a rue left to thicken in the saucepan.

Barb had driven them most of the way into Lito. Her grandparents owned their plot of shooting land there: six acres of thick pine forest fronted by barren crop fields that bellied up to the main drag. They'd taken the Wrangler because Barb's coupe didn't have trunk space enough for both the big meat cooler and the foam and plastic decoy, not to mention the rifles in the back seat. Now the clutch was giving Barb hell, and she was giving it right back. Her idea to learn—but now they were stalled out under the Shell station's lights while Barb tried to get her feet in sync. The Wrangler bucked and spat, and Joan watched her friend's face get redder and redder.

"It hates me," Barb snarled, smacking the wheel. Finally she let the engine die, and the following silence was undercut by the motor ticking cool. She let her head clunk against the headrest, looking slantways at Joan. "I lost the touch. Sorry, I guess."

"I thought you were getting the rhythm of it," Joan offered. "Took me a week to get out of first gear when I learned."

But Barb just shook her head. "It's not gonna happen. I can usually tell straight out whether I'll get something or not. And this..." She palmed the bulb of the shifter and grinned with half her mouth, showing snaggled teeth. "I'm fine driving automatic the rest of my life."

Joan thought back on a hundred such adventures, of Barb trying her hand at an eclectic reel of new skills: coding (an abject failure), free running (triumphant, despite a pair of ruined yoga pants and a pending trespassing charge), and now driving a manual transmission—also in the loss column. Joan knew better than to push the issue further. Barbara Cobb was the best quitter she knew, and Joan figured her mind was made up. She wondered how her friend had learned to hunt and shoot. Maybe this came on instinct, like for any true carnivore. Maybe it was inborn: how to track and kill and devour prey.

"You drive, Jones." Barb slid out the driver's door and stretched her hips. "We're pretty close now, I can guide you the rest of the way there."

Joan shrugged and clambered out into the cold. As she circled the Wrangler, a flash of movement caught her eye. A white flicker, almost luminous in the darkness on the other side of the road. One big doe picked up its head, then another. They stared at Joan with great dark eyes, their lop-ears flicking. Joan stared back. Then as if at some secret signal, the deer turned and bolted, bounding away until the dark swallowed them both.

"Look there, Jonesy!" Barb hollered, pointing.

"Is that a good sign?" Joan asked. She came around her side of the Wrangler and popped the door open, putting in one foot but not climbing in all the way.

"Hard to tell." Barb scratched her head where she'd just shaved her undercut back down to the scalp. "I've had it happen where I'll see twenty plus on the drive up—then not spot a damned thing once I'm posted up in the stand. That's a tough thing."

They got back in the Wrangler and pulled away onto the main road again. Joan's headlights pushed into the darkness, but there were no more deer on the roadside. Barb sat quiet in the passenger seat. One leg was pulled up on the seat cushion, and her hands were laced around her knee. Lights from streetlamps flickered in through the passenger window in steady rhythm, dousing Barb's form in shadow, then light, then shadow again.

Joan turned her attention back to the road. "If it's worth anything to you," she said, "I really thought you were getting the rhythm of it."

Barb pointed out the windshield. "There's our turn," she said, and that was all.

Ø

The Cobb ranch had no driveway, only a wide gravel path looping around the back of the house, wide enough for two cars to pass comfortably. Joan bumped the Wrangler up into the side yard, parking next to a long-hooded sedan and an empty tow-trailer rusting in some weeds. Beyond this, the empty field stretched out into infinite dark. Joan had seen a flash of the landscape they'd be hunting: furrows of earth nearer to the house gave way to dried corn stalks, weeds, and high wild grass, all rendered colorless in the Wrangler's beams. Somewhere behind these lay acres of woods, but they were hidden behind thick curtains of deep country darkness.

Barb's grandparents met them on the steps of the back deck. The grandfather was a tall man in corduroy pants and a plaid button-shirt that had been blue a hundred washes ago, barefoot despite the cold. His wife was shorter but still big for a woman, with red hair and broad red cheeks and dark clever eyes that glittered under the dusky deck lights. Barb got to them first, and they took turns yanking her into bearhugs and asking the usual questions about her hair and work and her old friends from college. Joan stood a few paces off, watching this clan greeting with her duffel slung across her shoulders. Finally they turned their eyes to her.

"You're Joan then." The grandfather's handshake was tight as iron. "The ad wizard."

Joan nibbled the inside of her mouth. "Barb told you, I guess."

"She told us you're good at what you do." It was the grandmother, answering for her husband with a flap of her hands. "And she told us you work for interesting people."

Joan opened her mouth, but before she could speak she got pulled into a sudden hug.

"We're glad you came up," the grandmother continued. "You'll call me Marjorie, and he's Ulysses—only, call him Yul. He's an old man and he can't remember three-syllable words."

From inside the hug, Joan heard the grandfather—Yul—give a derisive snort. Marjorie had a foot on Joan and smelled like flower petals and rain and kitchen spices. Her grip was just as firm as her husband's handshake had been. Joan wondered how Barb had wound up as short as she had, coming from a race of giants such as these.

"Thank you for inviting us," she said into Marjorie's gingham shoulder.

Yul cast his eyes around the deck, peering into the darkness pushing in around them. "My bones can't dig this cold," he said. "You young ladies eat anything on the trip in?" The girls shook their heads no, and he turned solemnly back toward the sliding door. He seemed to favor his right leg slightly, taking rolling steps to keep weight off it. "You come on inside then. Marjorie's got a hamburger casserole heated up, and I could stand a brew."

The warmth inside made Joan peel her hoodie jacket off and look for a hanger or chairback to roost it on. The ranch was small, with peeling linoleum in the kitchen and pale green carpet everywhere else. Beyond the kitchen lay a small warm den where a tube television squatted on a large trunk, playing some old sitcom on mute. The walls were wood-paneled save for the kitchen itself, which had bright blue wallpaper and a dark brick backsplash. Marjorie brushed past Joan and Barb, bustling into the cooking area and carrying out stacks of paper cups and plates. Yul loomed in a corner of the dining space. He'd opened a beer bottle using his shirttail and now there was a small dark stain in a line across his belly.

The hamburger casserole ran a little on the plate, but it was warm and stuck against Joan's ribs like home cooking could do. Soon she'd eaten two plates and was leaned back in her chair, her hand resting on her overfull stomach. The house was already too hot for Joan's blood, and the food and drink inside her made her skin feel flushed and feverish all over. Marjorie and Yul had grilled her on all the usual things, but when the subject of work came up she just smiled and bunted, or changed topics. Soon she faded into the background again, content to listen to the others' jabber. Yul kept pulling dark bottles of a beer Joan had never heard of before out of a cooler on the kitchen counter, and by the time Marjorie was putting a pie on the table, Joan was drinking her third. Now she had to pee, but Marjorie had just put a slice of the pie in front of her, so she didn't excuse herself. She ran a forefinger around and around the top of the bottle, looking at nothing and hoping her face wasn't too red.

"How's the herd, Pops?" Barb asked. She'd requisitioned another bottle of her own, and Joan watched her snap the lid off on the hard stone counter.

"Plenty of button bucks." Yul had poured his beer into a clear mug, which he swigged from and let his eyes roam across the popcorn ceiling. "Saw a few come along the southern treeline, but not close enough for me to count horns. Plenty of does too. Mike Pete called up the other day, talking about a line of turkeys he saw out in the back six, but he didn't shoot at them."

"You let him know we were coming in?" Barb caught Joan's eye and smiled. Joan shuffled her sneakers against the carpet beneath the table.

"Shore did," Yul replied. "Nobody's been in the woods for at least two weeks. The deer won't have a scent to spook them. Should be good shooting. You ever get a deer, ad wizard?"

Joan felt her chest knot up a little, her face flushing again. "Nope."

"We might fool around with the .22 some tomorrow," Barb cut in quickly. "Maybe get the shotgun out too, plink at some cans in the backyard. But the 30-30's got a sinister kick on it if you're not used to that kind of power. Joan's never held a gun before."

"Is that right?" Yul peered across the table over the tops of his glasses. His eyes didn't really find Joan. He just kind of stared over her shoulder a moment, then looked down into his mug. "Shame Liz couldn't make it up this time," he said with forced disinterest.

Barb got a funny look on her face. "Well, she's been so busy..." she began. "She's starting to get big commissions again. It's bad enough that she broke out the wrist brace."

"And there's planning the wedding too, of course," Marjorie added in a scolding tone. "Honestly, Yul." She slid something from beneath her placemat and held it under the chandelier. It was a bit of cream-colored cardstock with a silver foil design on the back of it. She twitched it between her fingers, then turned warmly to her granddaughter. "We were so thrilled when we got these in the mail. Did Elisabeth do the design on the back? That floral pattern?"

"No, they came like that." Barb stared down at her half-eaten pie. "Out of the box."

Joan stared at the card in Marjorie's hand. She'd missed it at first glance, but now she saw the words printed in the middle of the silver foil on the back. *Save the Date.* Under the table, her hands gripped her knees. Suddenly her throat felt very dry, in spite of the beer.

"I didn't know those had gone out," she said.

"Shore." Barb scratched her scalp. Joan could hear her nails scraping across the shaved surface; it was that quiet in that dining room. "About a week ago. Maybe a little longer."

Marjorie prattled on: "Well, we're just so proud of you both. All of us."

Here she turned her smile on Joan briefly, but Joan didn't meet her look. Her eyes darted across the room, looking for some safe place to rest her gaze. There in the den loomed something she hadn't spotted before: a mounted deer's head jutted out over the mantel, its horns branching up toward the ceiling. The buck's head was turned slightly at the neck, facing out toward the dining room as though it was listening in to the conversation at the table. The flickering from the TV set lit the huge hairy head from underneath; Joan could not see its glass eyes at that distance, only dark shapeless hollows hidden in the tufted fur. But it was looking straight at her.

"It's a very nice pattern," Joan said. "Even if Liz didn't make it. It's very nice." Then she stood, knocking her chair back against the buffet. "Marjorie... Where's a bathroom?"

"Down the hall on your right. Past that's the guest bedroom. Yul brought your things back." For a moment, the old woman's eyes had been wide and startled, but now she peered at Joan keenly, her gaze hooded and her hands folded under her chin. Yul kept staring into his mug of beer like he thought it would change color. Joan nodded her thanks and strode off around the corner. Barb called something after her, but Joan didn't quite catch all the words. Soon normal conversation resumed, and Joan closed the door behind her, shutting it all out.

Inside the tiny hall bathroom wasn't any cooler than the rest of the house. But Joan felt like she'd been holding her breath, and now she took in great gulps of hot stale air. A bulb in the sconce over the mirror flickered and spat, buzzing like an angry insect was trapped inside. Joan sat down on the fuzzy toilet seat and leaned her elbows against her knees. The ache in her bladder was gone for the moment, but it would come back. The walls of the bathroom were all papered over. Not blue like the kitchen, but a natural pattern, brown vertical lines like trees. Together, they made a forest surrounding her. For a brief moment Joan could see the darkness beyond those trees, slipping between them like something alive.

Beyond the door, the Cobb family moved around the house, cleaning up from dinner. Eventually Joan finished her business in the bathroom and rejoined them. Things had cooled inside the ranch house; outside, darkness crushed in from everywhere.

Ø

Then it was bedtime. The guest room was the house in microcosm: small and too warm, with two trundle beds made up with sheets with white flowers on them. A single lamp on a nightstand beside the second bed lit the space, and the window looking out at the side yard had no shade on it. Joan watched Barb lay her things out for the day to come. Neither girl said anything. Barb hung something on a hook in the small closet and shut the door on it, then started for bed. The blanket on Joan's bed was a patchwork quilt, and surprisingly heavy.

"You told me she hadn't decided yet," she said.

Barb stopped and looked at her, a startle playing out across her face. One leg was covered by the sheets; the other dangled to the floor. "I got surprised when you asked me about it," she replied at last. "I didn't know what to say to you."

"You said that because I spooked you?" Barb didn't answer. She lay back on the bed, the springs complaining, and stared at the ceiling. Joan nibbled her lip. "Well, what did she say?"

"She's not doing this to hurt you."

"Bullshit. You're my best friend. I should be there."

"I want you there. But things..."

"What things? What do 'things' have to do with this?"

"Things are complicated, all right? Everything's screwed up right now. Especially after the election. Liz feels...exposed. She's not sure how she feels about you right now."

"It sounds like she's pretty sure how she feels."

Barb set her mouth in a line. "All right," she said. "Have it your way." She sat up a little on the bed, watching Joan closely. Joan studied the pattern their feet had made on the carpet.

"She can't blame me for this," she said.

Barb shrugged, too casual. "You went to work for them. That was your choice."

"It's an agency job," Joan snarled. She sat forward, throwing aside a handful of blankets. "We work for whoever knocks on the door. I don't pick my clients, or the ads I get to write." She collapsed back against the wood paneling, her spite already spent up.

"Besides," she muttered. "It's not like we won."

"That's not what your guy is saying."

"Oh, Goddamn it—he's not 'my guy.' I didn't even work on that account."

"But still."

"But still, nothing." Joan peered across at her friend. Now Barb took her turn examining the carpet. Joan guessed she knew the pattern better. "Barb, what are you telling me?"

"This is between you and Liz."

"You're blaming this on me too?"

"I don't wanna get in the middle."

"Sure, you're not involved at all. All you're doing is marrying her."

Barb jerked her head in Joan's direction. Her dark glare flashed in the half-light. "That make you feel good to say?" she asked sharply.

Joan shook her head. "No, not particularly."

"Well—three guesses how it felt to hear."

A stillness followed. Joan eased down on her back, pulling a pillow under her head. The lamp made a circle of light on the popcorn ceiling. A crack ran from the center of the ceiling to the edge by the door, running along the angle between ceiling and wall until it vanished.

"Look," Barb said. "We're here, aren't we? I didn't pick sides."

"A few months ago, it would have been all three of us."

"I wanted some time. Just the two of us, like we used to do it. Before..."

She trailed off suddenly. Joan glanced over: her friend's eyes stared into space, at nothing. "Before what?" Joan asked in a half-whisper. She prayed Barb wouldn't answer. Another long stillness followed this, but not so long as before.

"Before the wedding, I guess," came the reply.

Joan said nothing to this. Barb reached out and pulled the cord for the lamp.

The room went dark, and that was all.

Ø

Joan was sure she wouldn't sleep. Even inside the house, the darkness seemed thicker, more congealed somehow. A few times she heard animals calling outside the window, sounding very close to the house. One was an owl, another was a barking dog. A few others she couldn't place: not growls or shrieks, but a coughing chuffing sound, somewhere between a tiger and a steam engine. Then there was just silence, and the hum of her thoughts.

Moments later, Barb was shaking her awake.

"Go on and get dressed," the dark shape of her friend whispered. "I've got some extra camo to go over your clothes. It's twenty-five degrees out right now."

Joan fumbled for the lamp. Her fingers found the cord and she clicked it. No light.

"Power's out," Barb explained, her voice farther away now. "Happens sometimes in the winter out here. I've tried to convince Pops to spring for a generator, but they like their piles of blankets, I guess. We'll have to dress in the dark."

Joan yawned and rubbed her aching jaw. Her eyes stung when she tried to open them. Slowly she forced herself upright and slid into the pants she'd left on the floor, then took the extra clothes Barb handed her. There was a bulky set of coveralls that came up to her collarbone and fastened like a bib, and a stiff canvas coat that fit over her hoodie jacket. If it was all camo-patterned, she'd have to check to see for sure once she was out in daylight. Next she fished her gloves out of her backpack and slipped them on, then followed Barb out the door.

The house was quiet and still pitch-dark save for a nightlight in the main hall leading to the den. The shapes of the furniture loomed like crouching forms. Joan felt the eyes of the hanging buck's head on her as they padded across the carpet. She didn't turn and look. Half-asleep, the thought of the head moving, following her footsteps through the house, shot hard nails of fear into her. Barb stopped by the kitchen table and knelt down, pulling something from beneath it. Joan saw that it was the case for the big deer rifle. Barb undid the latches and lifted out the weapon: it gleamed slightly in the half-light, especially on the dark oily muzzle. Holding the gun upright against her shoulder with one hand, Barb groped inside the case with the other for a moment, then shoved a handful of cold slippery somethings into Joan's hands.

"Here, fill your pockets up." Barb stood, heading for the door. "We probably won't need the extra rounds, but we'll be careful anyhow."

Joan slipped the bullets into the front pockets of the camo bib. They were heavy against her chest, but didn't make sound when she moved. "Barb...what we talked about last night..."

Barb stopped in the doorway. In the dark, her face had no expression on it at all. "We're getting an early start, so the deer won't be out," she said. "But they've got much better hearing than people do. Best plan is not to talk too much out there in the field."

Joan nodded silently. Yes, better not to talk at all. That was Barb, quitting again. "What should I do if I see a deer?" she asked. "That's what you said, that I should be your spotter."

"Whisper real low," Barb replied. "But don't point. They'll see that for sure."

Cold swept in through the open door. Joan shivered, then followed Barb outside.

Morning was coming on slowly there in the back field. The sky was pale gray and so was the earth below it. The only color streamed in from the east, where the first stripe of yellow sun was spreading like running eggs. The field was as Joan remembered from the night before: dried corn stalks, tall gray grass, and bare brown muddy earth in low furrows stretching out toward the forest. The trees themselves were a wash of dark ink, browns and blacks and greys, all running together. The world got darker closer to the treeline: it was as though the forest breathed in light, or breathed out the darkness itself. The trees formed a rough semicircle around the field and ranch house, like embracing arms. The air was cold and dry and ached inside Joan's lungs.

She followed the shape of Barb's back along a foot-worn path that paralleled the road, watching the tip of the rifle bob and twitch on her shoulder. Soon a structure came into view. Nestled in a small stand of trees and bushes on the eastern edge of the field was a metal platform on top of a small tower. The platform had a bench on it and two rung-like steps leading up to this, and there was a small black folding camp chair squatting beneath it. Barb pointed to the chair silently, then gestured to Joan, slashing the air with her hand like she was commanding a company of soldiers.

Joan moved sluggishly to her seat and eased down into it. The fabric was cold through the seat of the coveralls and slightly damp. Above her, Barb moved up the rungs onto the platform, making no sound. Joan had never seen her move like that before. Each movement of her arms and legs was precise and controlled, with no effort wasted. The rifle was clutched in one fist, so she had to climb using only one arm. Soon she was situated on the bench with the long gun balanced on her knees. Joan twisted around to look at her; Barb saw her looking and jerked her head out toward the open field. *Look. Watch.* Then she sat motionless, staring out toward the treeline.

Joan faced forward and followed her gaze. The world was still slate-colored all over, the color of dust hanging in a sunbeam. Nothing moved. The field was huge and empty, and there was no wind to move the tops of the dried stalks. She narrowed her eyes, looking for moving shapes at the edge of the treeline. There were no shapes. Once she saw a quick darkness swoop over the grass, but this was only the shadow of a hawk wheeling toward the forest. The cold numbed her skin, made her thoughts turn slow in her head.

Soon she stopped looking for deer at all. Pretty soon after that, she let her eyes close.

When she opened them again, Barb was climbing down out of the deer stand. The sun was much brighter now, warm against her skin. Barb's face was set in a grim mask, but when she looked at Joan she managed a wry smile. "Good morning, sunshine. See any deer?"

"Nope." Joan winced and rubbed her neck. "Sorry I sacked out. How about you?"

"Bupkis." Barb's voice was still quiet, despite the hour. "Thought I spotted something over that way, but it wasn't anything. Anyhow, I usually see more action in the evening. That'll be the better shooting, I bet."

There was a careful note in her friend's voice, Joan noticed. Something was hidden there. Something was being kept under tight control. Joan felt her heart sink. She searched Barb's face, but the other girl turned away, slinging the rifle over her shoulder.

"Let's get some breakfast," she said. "Me-Ma and Pops will be up by now, and Me-Ma's probably started cooking. Walk quietly, though—you can still see 'em this late sometimes."

She started toward the ranch house. Her step was heavier than it had been before; at least, Joan could hear the dry grass crunch under her feet now. There were still no cars on the nearby road, but in the far distance she could hear the sounds of engines. The lights on the back deck were lit, even if it was hard to tell in the brighter morning lights. The field was all lit up now in a yellow glow, and color had returned to it. Joan could make out nibbled-over ears of corn hidden in the wild grass. There too was the bright orange curve of a rotten pumpkin smashed in the mud. But the forest was still impenetrable. Along the treeline, individual trunks were discernible, but beyond that was all gray shadow.

"You smelling that, Jonesy?" Barb said from up front.

Joan didn't smell anything. She grabbed Barb's shoulder, stopping them both short. She pointed toward the treeline. One of the shadows had moved, taking a step onto the dead grass.

There was a deer standing at the edge of the field.

It was about forty yards off, standing in profile to the two girls, still half-in-shadow from the outcropping of the forest canopy. The deer was a doe and quite mature. Its fur was dark and its back was broad and rounded, and it stood completely still, its neck twisted to look back into the woods from where it had come. One ear flicked once, twice... Joan stayed as still as she could, hardly daring to breathe at all. Barb turned toward her, holding the rifle in both hands.

"What's the matter with you?" Her face was blank, and red with cold.

"There—by the treeline." Joan didn't dare point. Every movement of that heavy canvas coat rustled in her ears, and the doe's ears were so large. Surely it had heard them already? Smelled their scent? Seen them moving across the field toward the house?

Barb put the rifle up to her shoulder, looking down through the scope. The barrel swept along in a smooth slow line as she scanned the forest. "Where, Jones?" she whispered. "Give me a mark. What's it near, I don't see it."

"The trees make a kind of corner off to the left. It's in front of that. Can't you see it?"

Barb didn't answer. She only kept looking through the riflescope. Her finger drifted toward the trigger—then she huffed and lowered the gun. "It's not a deer," she grumbled.

Joan's hand dropped from Barb's shoulder. "Huh?"

"Take a look for yourself." Even with thick gloves on, Barb's fingers were nimble as she quickly unscrewed the telescopic scope from the top of the long rifle and handed it to Joan. "Look there, where you were pointing. The light's better on it now. Tell me what you see."

Joan put the sight to her eye and cringed. The metal was ice-cold against her skin. But as she looked through and focused in on where the doe had been...

"What am I looking at?"

"A log, sticking up at a funny angle. You're ghost-hunting, Jones. You wanna see a deer so bad, you make them up out of other things. Or out of thin air. I put a 30-30 round through a trash bag hung up in a tree once. Pops still tells the story."

Joan handed the scope back. "Jeez—I'm sorry. I really thought I saw one."

"Don't you go apologizing. I'm just glad you were awake this time."

But there was still something too careful in her voice. The jovial tone, the smile—it was all constructed. A facade, held up by leaning boards behind it. Behind them, the porch lights flickered. Marjorie appeared at the kitchen window, waving them inside.

"Let's go stand around some food," Barb said, already moving toward the house.

They went inside, but Joan paused in the back doorway, suddenly feeling strange all over. She felt like she'd felt when the stuffed buck's eyes had fallen on her. She turned back to the field just in time to see a flash of movement. The grass rippled once, like a burst of wind had washed over it. And the deer, the deer she'd seen only moments before, flicked its white tail and bounded away among the dark trees.

Ø

"Happy hunting, I hope?"

Marjorie put hot tea down on coasters in front of Joan and Barb, who sipped appreciatively. Joan had stripped off the heavy canvas coat and hung it over the back of the big recliner in the den, and both girls still had their boots on.

"I didn't hear shots," Yul murmured from behind a newspaper.

"Joan saw a ghost deer," Barb chirped into her tea. "Glad to see the power's back on."

Yul put down the paper and tweaked his glasses. "The garbage bag in the tree?"

"Not this time. Old rotten log by the treeline. Got me too, for a minute there."

"Huh. Well, if you're jumping at shadows now, you'll be in for a time come evening."

"What's that supposed to mean?" Joan asked, smiling. She was slowly getting over her embarrassment now, and the tea was making her warm all over.

Yul folded his hands. "Evening hunting's a whole other beast. Watching a field as the sun goes down, it's like watching a sunset. You can actually watch the shadows slip out from the treeline and come toward that deer stand in a line, like the tide coming in. The color drains out of the world—and that's when your mind starts playing games with you. You'll see plenty of ghost deer, sure, but what's screwy is the deer you don't see. Watching a field where nothing's moved in two hours...it hypnotizes you. You get locked in a pattern. And then you'll blink and there will be a deer standing right in the open. How did he get there? When did he leave the trees? You don't know. All you know is that you've got a rifle in your hands and the cleanest shot you're ever going to have all year. You know that buck belongs to you."

Joan glanced up at the stuffed buck on the wall. Now that light was coming through the windows, she could see the head's glass eyes more clearly. They were large and opaque and pointed in different directions. The whole head hardly looked real at all now. It looked artificial, like a child's huge plush toy. Barb followed her gaze, grinning over the rim of her tea mug.

"It's better with a spotter too," she said. "That's how you get the second deer, the deer you didn't see. The deer beyond the deer."

Yul nodded sagely. "Sometimes you can get two if you're quick enough. Sometimes the first shot doesn't even spook them, it just kind of freezes them in place. That's when you reload just as fast as you can while the gunshot's still hanging in the air. You can get them once they bolt, sure, but it's easier to shoot before that. Not everybody can hit a moving target."

"I could do it," Barb said, putting her mug on a coaster.

"You could do it," Yul agreed. "Barbara could do it. She shoots like I shoot."

He stretched, threw down his newspaper, and heaved to his feet. He was still wearing the same plaid button-up shirt he'd been wearing the night before, though the beer stain near his waist was gone. Joan wondered if he'd slept in it, or if he had multiples.

"Your Me-Ma's got some pan sausage ready," he said, scratching his stomach. Then he ambled toward the kitchen, heavily favoring his left leg.

Ø

Joan hadn't seen the field under open daylight. She'd only imagined it—but now she stood out in its center, feeling dry mud and dead grass crunch under her boots. The air was curiously warm. The sun was behind an all-gray sky and she couldn't feel its rays, but she was warm all the same, even without the thick canvas coat. The air was thickened somehow as well, thick like the dark had been thick before. Her movements were slow and languid; she held a hand up in front of her face and wiggled the fingers, watching an afterimage of those same digits move out of sync before rejoining the parent appendage.

In the distance she spotted the deer stand, now empty. She wondered, suddenly, if there might be deer at the forest's edge now—and like magic, she turned and spotted them at once.

There were two of them, moving slowly along the treeline. Both were does like she'd seen off the highway the night before. One had darker fur than the other, and this was the slightly smaller of the pair. Their bodies seemed thinner than deer Joan remembered seeing before, and their legs were longer, but what struck her most was how close they were to her. She was only forty feet or so away from them. Surely they knew she was there. But if they were aware of her at all, they showed no sign. They stepped along the shadow at the edge of the field, every movement as precise as clockwork.

Then, suddenly, they stopped. Both heads turned in unison—at first, Joan didn't understand they weren't looking at her. But when she heard voices coming from behind her, she followed their gaze: two figures stood in the backyard of the ranch house in the shadow of the deck. One of them was Barb. She was in her usual getup: faded green military jacket and Doc Martens, but her hair was longer, pulled back flat on her head and combed, and dark brown instead of its customary bright blue. The other figure was a girl as well. Elisabeth Arnold—Barb's Liz. Her blue dress, the one she'd been wearing the last time Joan spoke to her, was tracked with mud around the hem from the field, and her feet were bare. Joan couldn't see her face. Liz was turned at an angle, the sun catching her in such a fashion that her expression was unreadable. But Joan could imagine her face, how the expression was about to shift. She remembered this moment. Barb smiled nervously at her, then sank onto one knee in the mud.

Joan couldn't see Liz's face, but she could hear her. She could have heard her even from miles away. "Oh, Barbara, yes!" She threw herself into her fiancée's arms. "Yes, of course, yes!"

Joan spun away, eyes burning. She didn't want them to see her watching. She didn't want Liz to see her at all. Maybe she could circle around, make it inside the house before she was spotted. Maybe she could make the Wrangler, still parked in the side yard. Or she could vanish. The woods were at her back, cool and dark. She could live there like the deer and never come out. She turned toward the treeline—

The deer had come to meet her.

One slender-bodied doe had crossed the field between them and stood close to her, over her, standing high up on its back legs now, impossibly tall. It twisted its huge brown head around, fixing her with one wine-dark eye, then the other, like a bird of prey. Joan stood transfixed. The mud seemed to have closed around her boots. The voices from behind her faded, and all over there was great stillness. Everything was quiet. The doe craned its long neck down toward her. The mouth opened as if it would speak, full of flat brown teeth, yawning wider and wider...

$$\emptyset$$

She jolted awake, sliding half-off the armchair and nearly crashing against the tiled coffee table. Awareness came slowly. Her breaths huffed out in hot gusts. She could still see the doe looming above her, smell its breath as its jaws opened just above her skull. But slowly the world took shape around her again. There was the TV, the sofa, the hall.

Marjorie came bustling into the room, eyes wide. "I heard yelling. Are you all right?"

"I'm okay, I think." Joan picked herself up, feeling along her ribs where they'd scraped against the hard wood inside the arm of the chair. "I just...fell asleep again, I guess."

"You were drooling." Barb walked in, holding an armload of canvas grocery bags. "But I didn't want to wake you up. You have a bad dream or something?"

"I'm okay," Joan repeated. Looking at Barb was suddenly difficult. Instead she looked at the TV, which showed nothing but her own reflection. Her heartbeat still hadn't calmed down, and her breaths still came out heavy. The girl in the dark screen looked terrified.

"We gotta get some groceries for dinner." Barb hoisted the bags, jiggling them so they flapped. "Milk, eggs. Some white bread, I think. The basic food groups." She came around the side of the chair, looking at Joan curiously. "You sure you're all right? You're red all over."

Before she could react, Marjorie pressed the back of a hand to Joan's forehead. The old woman's skin felt strangely rough and stiff, pressed against her own. "Well—I don't think you're feverish. But drink some water just the same, before you two go out. If you're anything like Barbara, you'll forget water when it's cold out like it is now."

Joan shrugged and nodded thanks, then wandered off to the kitchen. The tap water tasted a little funny, but she drank two glasses of it standing by the sink. As she drank, she stared out the kitchen window across the back yard and corn-stalk field. Nothing moved among the trees.

Then she and Barb were in the Wrangler, winding along a country road to the Circle K. Barb had Maps up on her phone, and every so often their travel playlist would get interrupted by the polite voice of the navigator telling them when their turn was coming. Eventually the turns started coming so thick and fast that Barb shut the music off altogether.

"I didn't say it in the house," she said. "But we've gotta pick up a prescription for Pops too. He doesn't like people talking about it, but I thought you ought to know."

"Why?" Joan pulled into the parking lot, which was almost entirely empty. "Not that I care one way or the other. It's not serious, is it?"

"I don't know a lot about it. Me-Ma and him, they're pretty private about that sort of thing. But I know he's got good days and bad days. When you've talked to him, he's been doing pretty good. He's together, mostly. But earlier, while you were sleeping..."

She broke off suddenly, staring out the window. Joan followed her gaze only to realize that she was looking at nothing at all. She let the silence ride and said nothing.

Finally, Barb turned back toward her. "He said things I didn't understand. Odd things, frightening things. Most of it didn't make sense, but after a while..." She broke off again, but didn't look away. "I'd never seen him that bad. They ought to get somebody to come help them out at the house. Or they should move in with Mom and Dad."

"But he's stubborn?" Joan offered.

Barb shrugged. "He says nothing's wrong. There's no reasoning with him. Liz says it's not my job to fix it all but I can't put it down. Sometimes I can't think about anything else."

Joan chewed her lip. "Barb... I'm sorry."

Barb nodded, turning away sharply again. After a moment, she said: "He likes you, I think. Sometimes it's hard to tell with him, but I know he likes you. He's glad you're here."

Joan's hands frittered in her lap. With the engine off, the inside of the Jeep was getting colder by the second. She opened her mouth, shut it, and opened it again. She said: "Let's talk about last night a little. I can't leave that where we left it."

Barb blinked, as though she was coming out of a trance. "What's this?"

"About Liz. And the wedding."

Another blink, followed by a perplexed frown. "We talked about it at dinner—and then we went to bed. I don't remember anything else."

"You're joking. We..." Joan broke off, searching her friend's face. Barb gave her a blank look, giving almost nothing away. But she gave away enough. Joan twisted the key out of the ignition. "Have you got the list?" she said simply.

"Uh-huh." Barb tapped her phone. "Let's shake a leg. I want to have time to set up the decoy this evening. And maybe teach you how to shoot the .22."

"All right." Joan swung her legs out of the driver's seat. They bustled into the Circle K, cold whirling in after them, and did their shopping. Joan didn't talk about Liz again. She didn't talk about anything. She let Barb's conversation wash over her. Now she was a quitter too.

Ø

Early afternoon came. After an hour of pinging old soup cans in back of the house, the mud at the edge of the field was littered with .22 casings. Joan was getting a pretty good handle on the weight of the little pistol. Barb seemed pleased with this development: she kept making whooping cowboy noises every time Joan knocked a Campbell's can over on its side.

Eventually Marjorie came outside in a jacket and slippers, coming up to the edge of the deck. "Has the West been won yet?" she asked.

Barb scratched her scalp. "Getting there. Joan's pretty good with this thing. Might let her take it with us out to the stand this evening."

"Did you get Yul's prescription?"

"In the medicine cabinet in your bathroom. The rest of the groceries are all put away. How's he doing? I didn't see him when we went inside earlier."

Marjorie nodded, her glasses bouncing in her hair on the top of her head. "He's resting a little bit. He got real excited when you girls got here, and I think it wore him out."

Barb shot Joan a meaningful look. "We're not being too loud for him?"

"Yul sleeps through hurricanes. You girls are fine."

Barb nodded once and didn't say any more. She held out her hand for the .22 pistol, which Joan passed her—butt-first, like Barb had instructed her. Marjorie wandered inside, and Barb gave her a little wave over her shoulder. Then she put four holes into the empty soup can farthest from where they were standing. The shots weren't loud, only little pops. Joan wondered how the 30-30 would sound. Yul had talked about the shots hanging in the air. She thought of loud thunder, the kind that shook window glass in its frames, the kind that knocked you over.

Barb's last shot put the Campbell's can on its side, and Joan tried to imitate her friend's cowboy whoop. She thought she did all right, but there was something hollow in the sound. The hollowness came from in her chest, from some cavity inside her. Joan pulled her hoodie around herself. The hollowness yawned. She couldn't shake it.

Night would be coming on soon. Now Barb was picking around in the weeds under the deck for stray casings, and Joan excused herself inside. The cold was seeping under her skin, numbing her all over and making her hands stiff. A crack had opened across the knuckles on her right hand, and she went to the kitchen sink, running the water until it was hot enough to warm her. The house was quiet, save for the hum of the furnace under the floor and the slight murmur of the television set. Yul was asleep on the couch; his mouth was open as though he were snoring, but he made no sound as his chest rose and fell. Marjorie was nowhere to be seen.

Joan ran both hands under the warm water, then shut the faucet off abruptly. She listened. There—she heard another soft thump, coming from the bedrooms, followed by a strange grunting sound. Joan shook her hands dry over the sink and wiped them on her jeans. She peered through the kitchen window: Barb was still crouched somewhere near the back deck. She could see her blue undercut, bobbing just beyond the slats of the railing. Joan wandered toward the western wing of the ranch house, through the dusky den and toward the hall. Yul had not stirred from his slumber. The house was quiet again, nearly completely silent.

She found herself in front of Yul and Marjorie's bedroom door, which was half-ajar. The hall was dark, but a little light seeped out through the opening and under the crack below the door. No noise came from behind it. Joan listened, nearly pressing her ear against the wood.

Something thumped. Something grunted.

Joan froze. Nothing moved beyond the door—nothing came storming through, snorting and frothing. She toed the door open, her arms wrapped tight around herself... She had never seen the inside of this bedroom before. Inside was the same green carpet as everywhere else, the same dark wood paneling, the same worn furniture. Marjorie was on the floor behind the door, half-behind the big four-poster bed. She was on all fours, not on her hands and knees as though she had fallen, but kind of splayed out, with every limb locked as though she were trying to stand up from that position. But she did not stand. She was completely still. Her head was hidden behind the drape of the bedskirt.

"Marjorie...?" Joan's voice came out too soft, hardly a whisper.

The old woman's hand rose up, gripping the post of the bed in a tight-knuckled fist. Then she stood, smiling. Something glittered in her other hand.

"Joan, dear—you startled me. I didn't hear you walk up."

Joan hugged herself, feeling flushed. She looked down at the carpet. "I'm sorry. I heard a... I mean, I thought you might have fallen."

"You're so sweet." Marjorie's cheeks crumpled. "No, I'm all right. I just dropped my cheaters behind the bed there, see?" She waggled the object in her right hand: the glasses glinted in the light streaming through the blinds at her back.

"Oh. All right then."

Marjorie flashed a cat-like grin. "I can't believe you were going to come check on me. That really is sweet. Are you and Barb going back out soon? It'll start getting dark any minute."

Joan turned down the hall. The side door's hinges complained; Barb must have come back inside. "I think so," Joan replied. "We're getting an earlier start—to get the decoy set up."

"That's right." Marjorie slid her glasses onto her face and rubbed the side of her neck. "Make sure you use the pheromone spray. It's in the little cabinet beside the kitchen door. They can smell much better than they can see, you know. Much better than us."

Joan blinked. "The deer?"

"Yes, of course. The deer."

Joan nodded, unsure of what else to say. Down the hall, she heard Barb calling for her—softly, so she wouldn't wake Yul. Joan bobbed her head toward where Barb was, making an apologetic expression at Marjorie. The old woman folded her hands on the bedpost.

"Go on, then. Get us a big one. And don't forget what I said about the spray." Joan nodded again, but before she got too far down the hall, Marjorie called after her again: "You don't need to worry so much, Joan. We'll be all right, all of us."

Joan nodded again. She still couldn't think of a reply.

"We're just glad you're here," Marjorie said.

The old woman's glasses were covered by a glare, and her face gave nothing away.

Ø

"I had the strangest conversation with your grandmother just now."

They were digging the doe decoy out of the trunk of the Wrangler, wrestling with its bulk. Joan had her hands around the back legs, while Barb had gotten her arms around the thing's neck. The decoy had become wedged on the journey, and unsticking it was taking some effort. At their feet, a small bottle of scentant lay on its side. The air wasn't dark yet, but there was already deep shadow along the edge of the treeline. Night would fall quickly here.

Barb wrestled the decoy free at last and looked quizzically at Joan. "What's this now?"

"Well, I guess it wasn't so strange." Joan shrugged, setting her end of the foam-and-plastic doe on the gravel. "Only, I'd just found her on the floor. But she played it off like... I don't know. There was a vibe, I guess. A funny one."

"Was she hurt? Had she fallen down?"

Joan shook her head. "She said she was fine. But...I don't know. After what you said about Yul—your grandfather... I'm overthinking it, I guess."

Barb frowned, the expression warping a little under the fairy lights on the back deck. "Maybe not. I've been a little worried about her too. I think she might be a little malnourished or something. Did you feel her skin? When she hugged you the other night?"

"Her skin?"

"She cooks all day and never eats enough herself. Look, I don't mean to make this your problem. But I'm glad you told me what you saw. I really appreciate it."

Joan looked up toward the clouds. They covered the sky totally, showing nothing through. "I don't mind you talking about it," she said.

Barb was silent for a long moment. Joan kept looking at the clouds. Barb said: "I'm sorry I'm so bad at this. I don't know what to say to you. It's like the words aren't there."

Joan gave her friend a measuring look. "You're doing all right now."

But Barb had fallen silent again. Joan steadied her hands on the rump of the doe-decoy. Despite the difficulty they'd had getting it out of the trunk, it had been lighter than she'd expected it to be. The decoy wasn't solid; the legs were hard plastic all the way through with rubber skin, but the torso had a hollow in it—for easier transport, Joan guessed. She wondered how heavy a dead deer's body would be, all limp weight, slick with fresh blood. She wondered what it would be like to carry it back to the ranch house, slung between Barb and herself. She wondered how it would be to carry it alone.

"Just talk," she murmured, mostly to herself. "Just say anything you want to say."

Barb hoisted the long 30-30 onto her shoulder. "Remind me when we get back, I promised I'd give Liz a call. I missed last night, I guess I was too tired." She gave Joan a lingering look, pursing her lips. Then the moment was over. "You've got the decoy, Jones," she said. "We'd better get out there. It's gonna start getting dark any second." And that was all.

Ø

The decoy wasn't hard to set up. Barb angled it toward the deer stand maybe fifteen yards off and stuck its plastic feet into the mud, securing it. Joan spritzed some of the scentant onto the decoy's undercarriage, where Barb showed her. The stuff that came out was clear and didn't smell like much of anything to Joan, but her nose was full of mucus from the cold. Nothing smelled like much of anything to her just then. Now it was like it had been before: Barb was up on the high bench in the stand, with the 30-30 lying across her bent knees. Joan was again in her folding chair, only this time she had the little .22 pistol laying snugly against her hip, loaded with a single shot. The metal was cold, even through the thick canvas pants Barb had lent her, but there was something thrilling about having the weapon so close to her.

"It's not for hunting, really," Barb had explained to her. "The .22 probably won't bring down a button buck, much less a full-grown adult deer, even if you hit it center of mass. It's for wounded prey only—right between the eyes. Gut-shot deer struggle on for a long time. It's a sad thing. Sometimes they even limp off to bleed out in their own private places. They don't know they're going to die. They don't know the hunt is already over. Do you get it?"

Joan had said she did, even if she wasn't sure it was really true. But the idea twisted pain into her gut, so she nodded and hoped Barb wouldn't talk about it anymore.

"It's wasted pain," Barb had said, "and it makes the meat taste like shit."

Night was coming on—dark crept unyielding across the sky. But in the field there was still plenty of light coming over the tops of the trees. The dried grass and jutting cornstalks were a gray ocean, like a frozen pond or the surface of the moon. There was still some color, some leftover orange day-glow striping the grass nearest to the deer stand. But this was slowly shrinking away, being pushed aside by advancing country darkness. Long shadows threaded like fingers out from the treeline, reaching toward where the girls sat. Barb perched motionless above Joan, her rotating head scanning in endless arcs. Joan sat very still. The little .22 pistol was in her lap. She was not going to cost Barb a deer by moving, by making sound. She was not going to fall asleep again.

The hollow, sucking feeling inside her had come back. It returned suddenly, without warning or cause. She cast around inside herself to learn the source of the ache, but there was no source to be found. It felt like panic—it was quick and throbbing, making her heart beat fast. Even through the thick canvas overcoat, she was suddenly cold all over. The cold went right on down to her core, where it nestled and squirmed. She twisted her neck around, slowly-slowly-slowly so she wouldn't make noise: there above her, Barb still crouched, a dark form against the graying sky. The metal of the gun across her knees did not gleam. She was darkness all over, only half-corporeal. She was almost part of the night sky itself.

What had she said before? *I wanted some time with my best friend. Before the wedding.*

And what would come after? Night was falling heavy and fast—soon that country darkness would come for them again, and deer or no deer they'd have to go back inside the house. Morning would come, and she and Barb would drive back into town, back to their separate apartments and separate lives. This moment, whatever it represented between them, would be over. Joan could not see further than that. There, too, was darkness.

Yul had told the truth. The empty field *was* hypnotizing. Joan turned her head back toward the treeline in time to see the last real daylight fade. Now there was only a layer of dull orange spread across the treetops, like melting cheese running down. If she squinted, she could actually see the shadows creeping closer and closer to where she sat. They were a hundred yards, now eighty... It wasn't like a tide at all. There was no ebb and flow. It was a steady, inexorable march toward the road. Now it was only seventy yards from the tips of her boots.

Joan stole another look back at her friend. Barb had not stirred. Joan thought she heard her sniff the air, but this might have been mucus as well. She turned back and stared out across the jagged surface of the field. Her eyes strained against the gathering dusk, but nothing moved except the advance of the darkness. The hollow decoy stood resolute, facing the road. It would take all comers. Nothing moved. Nothing ever moved.

And then something did.

Joan sat forward on the camp chair suddenly. It took all her strength not to gasp, to stand up and point. There were two dark shapes out in the tall dead grass now. One was the decoy, still standing with its snout pointed straight toward her. The other stood about five yards back from this, flicking its ears in the darkness. It stood in profile, a perfect silhouette even in the new gloom. There could be no mistake this time. It was a deer, a real live deer.

Joan stared. Yul had warned her, but the magic trick still amazed her. How had it managed to sneak up on them? Which direction had it come from? The treeline was so far away, and Joan had not taken her eyes off the field. How had such a big animal made no sound on the dry grass? The deer was a doe, but still huge. The doe scent on the decoy should have had no effect on it—and yet it took step after careful step toward them, lifting dainty hooves to prod the ground, moving with incredible precision. It came closer and closer: soon it was near enough that Joan could nearly look in its eyes. Her heart beat hot and fast inside of her. Surely this too was an illusion. It *must* be a trick of the light, a bush, a shadow. But Joan heard Barb lean forward too, sucking in a single eager breath. She heard the heavy metal chunk of her friend chambering a round in the 30-30.

The deer's head perked up. Joan's breath hooked in her chest, but the beast didn't bolt. It simply twisted its neck around, looking toward the stand of trees where the girls lay hidden. An incredible stillness lingered over everything. Seconds crawled by...

The crack of the shot tore the world in half.

Joan clapped her hands over her ears. The booming sound hung in the air, echoing back from across the field. The doe twitched, jumped—suddenly it was dancing toward the ground, its four legs flying upward. One hoof struck the head of the decoy, sending it sprawling into the grass. Then it lay still and kicked no more. Joan's heartbeat roared in her ears. She almost didn't hear it when Barb jumped to her feet, shaking bark shavings down from the platform.

"Hot damn, Jones!" her friend hissed. "Good spot! *Great* damn spot!"

"I almost missed her," Joan heard herself say through chattering teeth. "I almost..."

"I didn't see her at *all*," Barb crowed. "But you leaned forward—and there she was, sniffing around Clarice there. Don't know what she wanted with a doe decoy though. But whatever. Come on, we don't want to lose her in the grass."

Barb was already scuttling down the rusty ladder, sending down more bark shavings that stuck in Joan's hair. Even in the dark, her friend's face glowed. Joan felt the hollowness in her shrink back. The initial shock of the gunshot had worn off, but that old ache didn't sweep in to replace it. She didn't know what she was feeling now. Barb came up behind her and put her gloved hands on either side of Joan's head, gripping the chair back. Her friend peered over her shoulder, looking out into the darkening field.

"Shit—did you see where she fell? I can't see the decoy anymore, it's already too dark."

Joan pointed. "There, I've got it. See that clump? Look where I'm pointing."

"It's all clumps, Jones." Barb shook her head, grinning ecstatically. "You sit there a minute. Let me know if I'm getting close. We'll play hot and cold with her." She started off into the grass, then suddenly turned, looking at Joan like she would speak again. She stood like that with her mouth hung open no longer than a moment. Then she was off again, taking high strides so her boots cleared the stiff dry scrub. Each step crunched like ice. The 30-30 was slung over her shoulder now, and the stock bumped against her backside.

Joan called after her, "Will you need the pistol?" But Barb waved her off.

"I'll let you know," she hollered back. "I don't think—never mind, I see them now. There's the decoy... Holy shit! She's huge! Jonesy, you gotta see this! She's..."

Joan half-rose from the camp chair, then stopped. A movement off to her left had caught her eye: the fairy lights strung across the ranch house's back deck had begun to swing slightly, moving like they'd been pushed by a gust of wind. All the rest of the lights inside the house were on—but suddenly, one by one they clicked off. Only the fairy lights remained twinkling, swaying and swaying. Joan felt strange all over. She moistened her chapping lips.

"Barb?" she called out. "Barb?"

Ø

Maybe you think I can't hear you, Joan.

Maybe you think I don't listen when you talk; maybe you think I'm quitting out on you. I can figure that, I guess. I told you a fib just now—or was it the night before? I told you the words were getting harder for me. I told you they wouldn't come out like I wanted them to.

Here's my only truth: I'm all crowded up with words. I'm gummed up with them, like a wax statue. I've got so many words I'm afraid to open my mouth, that the wrong ones will come crawling out. The ones I don't mean. Or the ones I mean now, but won't tomorrow. I'm in a hard spot, but I won't spread that pain to you. Or I thought I wouldn't. But you picked it all up anyhow, didn't you? I thought I'd save you, but you never wanted to be saved.

Can you think back four years? Two? Six months? Who are those faces in the mirror now? You and me and Liz—we all changed so sharply, but I thought we'd kept ourselves. But now, a gulf yawns. It was the same bump in the road that sent us all three sprawling. But here I am on one side of this divide, and there you are on the other. Can you hear me from where you are? Can you see me waving? I won't ever tell you what Liz said. I can save you from that. That's all I can do now, is keep my mouth shut. That's how I can love you now.

And I do love you—and I don't love everything about you. But you're my best friend.

And I love Liz—and she's not perfect. But she's home.

Those are the points pulling me between them. I'll never choose one or the other, even if it would relieve that pressure. Liz wouldn't ever force that choice on me. I don't think you'd make me either. That's *my* choice, to believe this. But when I look out in this darkness, I can't see you. Jonesy—I'm afraid. But I'm not afraid of what might happen in the future. It's what's already happened that's got me spooked. Whatever the horror is, it's already begun. It's waiting for us at home. The rot has set in, somewhere damp and secret. But I won't look for it. Even if it means the floor gives out under us all, I won't sniff that rotten old board out.

You think I can't hear you, Joan. I hear just fine. Even the echo is loud enough.

Ø

The footsteps across the dry cold ground had gone quiet. Joan turned back to the field, looking for her friend. But there seemed to be a blank space left in the air where Barb had stood.

She was gone.

For the first instant, Joan was only confused, sure Barb was playing some prank. Or else she had just crouched down below the top of the dry scrub, examining her kill. But as she peered across the sharp points of the colorless grass, pinpricks of apprehension started crawling across the backs of her hands like many-legged insects. She looked left and right: no Barb. No moving girl-form against the dark wall of trees at the field's edge. She thought to call out to her friend, but something stopped her before she cupped her hands to her mouth. Some prey instinct twinged—a scent on the wind? A rustle in the grass? But there was no wind. There had been no sound, not even a branch breaking underfoot. The field looked like it had looked when they had first arrived. Like it had been empty forever, abandoned forever.

Joan's gloved hands gripped the arms of the folding chair. She stared across the grass, weighing options against each other in her head. She'd sat there shivering—how long now, exactly? A minute? Five minutes? The light from the Cobb house seemed so far off now. The once-warm orange light from the dusty back-porch bulbs looked like it was coming to her through deep dark water. The world all around her seemed huge and empty: through the trees, stars popped out in the dark sky one by one, their light cold and weak and impossibly far away.

She knew what had to come next. She would have to stand up and walk out on that field. She would have to go where Barb had stood, where dead or dying deer lay. The thought numbed her limbs worse than the cold. What would she find, pressing down the grass? She imagined her flashlight beam swooping along the grass, coming to rest on a bloodied flank—or on the head of the deer, lying on its side, its eye dark and open and glistening. But first she would have to walk there, pick her way across that crunching grass in the middle of that open field, under the weight of that huge dark sky. The dark was thicker here. She would have to swim through it.

She could imagine being the deer. Sniffing the air at the forest's edge. Staying motionless, listening for sound, any sound, drifting on the wind. Probing out with one tentative hoof, then another onto the grass, moving fitfully forward—almost in slow-motion, frame by tedious frame. Moving farther and farther away from the safety of the trees, ears twitching, every nerve pulled tight as whipcord... Joan imagined the hunger in the deer's belly, gnawing. Sometimes there was corn in the field. Sometimes a spill of grain. But these could be traps, decoys. The predator was cunning and just as hungry. So before you ate, before you put your head down low where you couldn't see and couldn't hear—you had to know it was safe. You had to be certain the predator wasn't lurking in that grass, or at the edge of the trees, waiting until you made yourself vulnerable. This was real fear. This was real terror—dumb animal panic.

The kind that keeps you alive. The kind you cling to.

Joan steeled herself, ready to press off the arm rests and stand—then stopped. Out in the open field, there had been movement. The top of the grass had rippled once, in a kind of wave across the entire pasture. It started where Barb had been standing, where the deer had fallen. Joan watched this movement surge over the dry scrub, moving away from her, toward the treeline. It was like a sudden wind had moved the grass in this singular line, like a path through the field.

But there had been no wind.

And now the dark form of a doe stood out against the trees on the other side.

Joan felt her skin go numb all over her body. There was no way to know for certain if this was the same deer she'd seen earlier in the morning. It was hardly a deer-shape at all at that distance. It was a silhouette, and its outline seemed to bleed out into the shadows behind it. Only the flick of its ears, the subtle movement of the head gave the game away. No—surely it could not be that same deer. But now Joan was imagining its flank bleeding from a single bullet hole, leaking shadow-dark fluid out onto the thirsty ground. The doe watched her across the field, completely motionless, nearly vanishing against the night.

Then it dipped its head down, as if to feed. When it raised it again, something dangled from its mouth. The distance made it impossible to see for sure what trailed from the doe's jaws. But Joan knew it was an arm. She imagined the creature—*not the deer, she would not call it a deer now*—turning, vanishing slowly into the trees, dragging by that same arm the limp body of her friend. She imagined Barb's dark eyes still open to the sky, still peering after the kill. But the doe-thing did not move at all. It watched her steadily, impossibly motionless.

Joan flicked her eyes over to the lights of the house. They were still on, a beacon set against the void of that cold night. Her hand moved slowly, slowly, slowly to the .22 pistol that had slid down beside her hip on the folding chair. There it was, the butt reassuringly cold against her fingers. She did not want to have to run for those lights. She would move slowly, the way the deer had moved. Probing movements, smelling the air, letting fear guide her forward. If she ran, then the creature would give chase—on instinct, she figured. She imagined that dark form on the forest's edge breaking toward her, not bounding like a deer but simply sprinting, steady and low and impossibly fast... But she could not stand up. She could not even move enough to wrap her hand around the butt of the pistol.

Something had rustled in the bushes only a few feet behind her. Something drew a deep, hoarse breath into un-human lungs. Something lay still and secret.

The doe at the edge of the woods had not moved, had not taken its eyes off Joan. She remembered what Yul had told her, about how the open field could hypnotize you. How you could miss a deer even when you were looking for them. But with a spotter, you could sometimes see the second buck or doe—the deer beyond the deer. Sometimes you got two, if you were lucky. If you had another pair of eyes. If you were patient and kept quiet.

Joan wouldn't turn. She sat very still, and the cold tightened and tightened across her. She could never be so motionless as the deer. Not even as still as Barb, perched on the stand with the 30-30 across her legs. But she could try it. She could hold her breath and pray, pray the shivering didn't give away the game. Maybe it wouldn't keep her safe—but it might stop the poisonous fear spreading inside her. She wouldn't dare run toward those lights now, would she? They were just another trap now, another decoy meant to draw her out of safety. But what was safe for her now? Barb was gone, perhaps she'd always been gone. And Joan remembered how Marjorie's hand had felt against her brow. Rough and thick-skinned, all too stiff. Like rubber, like foam. Not like human skin should feel at all. Slowly the thick blanket of darkness spread from the trees toward her, across her, leaving the field in full shadow at last.

The .22 still lay by her hip, loaded up with its single precious shot. The idea of fleeing, of hearing that hoarse whispering breath behind her growing louder and more excited with every step, filled her belly with cold, heavy fear. It was almost too much to bear. What would Barb have chosen if their positions were reversed? Had being prey come as easy to her as being a predator? Or had she quit out again, unwilling to commit to yet another losing proposition, to stand that black oozing terror any longer than she absolutely had to?

Had she fought? Had she struggled for her life—or simply let the kill come?

Behind Joan, the second creature let out another hoarse and quivering breath. It was waiting for something. A signal on the wind, or simply for Joan to bolt. Incredibly—in that moment, her thoughts flew to Liz, waiting a hundred miles away for a phone call that wasn't going to come. Barb wasn't coming home. Barb wasn't anywhere. Perhaps she could forgive Liz now, it would cost her nothing. It would make no difference at all. Instead, she broke away from the trees, crashing across the tall grass and leaving the pistol on the ground by the camp chair.

Nothing followed behind her. No hoarse breaths, nothing slavering out from the underbrush. There was only a soft whispering sound, a ripple running across the field toward the house. It was like a small gust of cold wind, even if there was no wind.

Joan had never been any good at quitting.

She broke hard for the back deck lights. She made it a good long distance.

The doe at the edge of the woods had not moved, had not taken its eyes off Joan.

The Machete at the End of the World

It was ten teenagers, forty years ago. I killed them (opened them up, spilling them onto wet sand, hard cracked sidewalk, creaking boardwalk planks) over a neat two-week span. This was 1979, in the summer. I got a name later on, a man's name, monosyllabic and blunt like a blow from a fist. But first I was just Tall Man, credited at the end of the feature. I don't remember their faces now. Only the color of their blood. Only the shrieks, like blasts on a whistle, like ten tracks on an era-perfect pop album.

I remember, too, the Halloween masks of my shark-chewed face. These came later on—and my dockworker duds, my rusted boatman hook, all costumes and plastic props hung from racks in dollar stores across a world that can't bleed anymore.

They didn't forget me, not even at the end. That's better than love, I think.

It's twilight now; it's nearly always twilight these days. Months, years. I'm stalking down some Point Pleasant back alley. I've still got that smooth-as-butter SteadiCam glide. I don't run, but I get where I'm headed. Now, that's nowhere. Detritus blows by my heavy boots. Tatters of napkins, a surgical mask, a wrapper off a condom, like tumbleweed, end over end over end. A year ago—the world, the living part of it, burned away. But I couldn't burn. When everything else died, I simply sat up.

The sky overhead is blood; burned, like the earth. Like the corpses I find sometimes even now, here and there. And the days are shorter. Darkness falls fast through smoke and atmosphere dust. My lungs are full of grit. That dark used to be home: I could move so quickly through it, silently, like I could swim in it submerged. Now the shadows expel me, push me out. There's nobody to see me, or not see. A dead world can't be killed.

Maybe sometimes people are born unglued. Empty, sort of. Missing a piece. I think I got the wrong piece put in by mistake. A kind of engine inside that pushed me forward, faster than a beating heart. It made me stalk and kill; it made it pleasurable to stalk and kill. I wonder if those teenagers could hear the engine going...churning behind my ribs, shunting off heat, burning through gallons of black oozing fuel.

Stalking forward. Coming for them.

Or maybe it was just my footsteps, heavy in rubber-soled boots.

I wonder if she heard the same thing. She was the last of them all, and the cleverest.

She got a name too, in the sequels. In the VHS release of the original as well. But I'll always know her as Last One, the name beside this in the credits lost to time's distortion. The last one on her feet, the last one drawing breath—it fits. The others got names and higher billing at first, but they offered themselves to me. Blood sacrifices on taut young legs. Not her. She was anonymous and deadly. I loved her for that.

It was sewing scissors, the first time. Through my one good eye with a sharp twist of the hand. Then a sparking electrical wire to the heart. Then a pond covered with ice, trapping me beneath. Then a charge of dynamite. A blazing inferno in my childhood home. A medieval sword. Helicopter blades. The jets from a spacecraft. Each time, I remember her relieved sobs or hysterical laughter. Laugh, my darling. It's over.

Then I sat up. I came back for her, over and over. That's better than love too.

It's night. The dark is hostile, blinding. I'm at the end of the pier; the water has a single constant metallic gleam all across the surface. It barely seems to move. I'm slower now. Slower moving, slower thinking. The engine in my chest chugs at half power. My fingers are stiff around the rusty hook. I wonder if the water would take me. If I would sit up—not at the silty bottom, but in some new Point Pleasant. A world that wasn't burned. A breathing world. A world alive, that could scream and bleed. I imagine it behind shut eyes.

But I'm not alone. For the first time in days, months, years, that old alarm trips. She's at the other end of the pier. I can't see a face. I don't need to see a face. There's nobody else. The world is dead, save her. Save me. The Last One—and a machete with a chewed face and heavy boots. She approaches, calling out. There's hope in her voice as sweet as any scream. And I'm approaching her too, my stride lengthening, slipping easily through the dark, SteadiCam smooth. We'll meet in the middle, closing, closing.

I don't know when she sees my face. When the dark is no longer blinding, her eyes are already bugging in terror. But she's still coming toward me on sheer inertia. Or maybe I'm catching up. Maybe I'm pursuing. Stalking, hunting again. The horror on her face, it shaves the years away. The engine roars hot inside me and the music blares a single terrible pipe-organ chord, and I'm raising the hook over my head—

Scream for me, my darling. Scream like an encore, a bonus track on the record. Don't call it a sequel. Call it a reunion, and a conclusion. I've come back for you. The world couldn't burn us. Listen to my heart, rumbling and roaring in me. Know that every cut, every drop of blood we spill together—it's a command, a plea. Under the soundtrack it repeats.

Love me. Love me. Love me.

Notes about These Stories

And now—if you'll permit me a little self-indulgence...

Nostalgia
For about a week, all I had was that first sentence. Eventually I forced myself to discover what the garden of hands meant and what became of it, and the result was "Nostalgia." This is a story about all the strange half-remembered parts of our childhoods, the stuff we can't quite believe—but have the scars to prove it really happened. How do these phantom scenarios shape us? And if they were so vital, why can't we *really* remember them?

First appeared in Tales of Sley House 2021, *Sley House Publishing.*

You Are the Hero of Legend
Like "Nostalgia," for a while all I had was the title. I've always been drawn to stories with a full sentence as a title, and this declarative sounded vaguely threatening. Once I came up with the Arthurian bent to the story, the rest wrote itself fairly easily. I've always been obsessed with the concept of persona, and the idea of hero-as-parasite was a pretty thrilling one, I felt.

First appeared in Issue IV, *Noctivagant Press.*

Song of the Summer
This was originally written for a beach-themed anthology prompt, a setting I'd never written anything about before. The idea of a haunted seashell came to me almost immediately, but the emotional core of the story—the past friendship between Cameron and Shanna—arrived slowly over the course of the writing. The shell

was always meant to be a red herring, but the idea for a *Fight Club*-style twist ending came from a colleague at work. Looking back on it, I'm not sure the story would have worked without it.

First appeared in Summer Bludgeon, *Unnerving Reads.*

Mister Mickenzie
Sometimes I'll start a story where I only have a single scene formed out in my mind. "Mister Mickenzie" was one such venture—and the scene in question is the moment Laura discovers the girls in their faux-sacrificial chamber. The rest formed outwards from this central radiating point, which explains why the story is told out of order. I've also always had a peculiar fear of inanimate, unjointed objects that move; the terror here is wholly my own.

First appeared in All Dark Places 3, *Dragon Soul Press.*

Some Bad Luck Near Bitter Downs
I don't know what precisely inspired this one. But there's a *Creepshow* quality to it that probably belies its origins. This is a pretty simple karma story, horror for horror's sake—but I'm quite fond of the final image we get of the monster fully realized. This is also the only non-flash story I've ever written where none of the characters who speak are given names.

Original to this collection.

The Panic
Another anthology-prompt story, this time for a "found footage" horror collection. I've always loved the idea of epistolary stories, especially those posed as "discovered documents" in an archive or web forum somewhere. I imagine that narratives like the account of "The Panic" probably litter the dark corners of cyberspace, waiting to be discovered.

First appeared in I Cast You Out!

1855
Another epistolary yarn—and my favorite in the collection, followed closely by "Song of the Summer." But ultimately I don't have a lot

to say about it other than: read it. Once I discovered the existence of Victorian "hidden mother" photography, I knew it was a frightening enough image to build a story around. Outside of the research I did to get the historical details (mostly) correct, this one pretty much flew out of me. I'm quite proud of it.

First appeared in Godless, *D&T Publishing.*

A Real Likeness

This is the only story in the collection that's connected to anything else I've written; eagle-eyed readers will probably spot that the two non-narrator characters in the account are Lutz Visgara and Kait Brecker from *The Unwelcome.* This was originally written as a companion story to appear in subsequent editions of that novel; instead, it appears here. Lutz is my favorite recurring character to write, as his motives are so alien and yet always pretty clear and open. And I really enjoyed imagining how an outsider to the novel's events might view a creature like Kait. There are also some pretty strong Lovecraft influences here, specifically from "Pickman's Model," which is where I drew the idea to make the nameless, doomed narrator an artist from.

First appeared in Night Terrors Vol. 20, *Scare Street Publishing.*

Copilot

Another attempt at exploring the "parasitic persona" idea introduced in "You Are the Hero of Legend." I first published this story in college, and aside from a few changes to the wording I've tried to preserve it as best I can here, warts and all. I think I actually wrote this for a science class of some kind—apologies to whatever professor I turned this in to.

First appeared in Liquid Imagination Magazine *as "Memories from a Distant Star."*

Red Meat

Something I've resolved to never do again: publish a story under any name other than my own. But at the time of writing, even the quasi-political nature of the story's subject matter frightened me, so for the first and only time in my career, I gave myself a quite ridiculous pen name when I went to publish it: *Jalopy Greer*. Fortunately for honor and good taste's sakes, the original outlet has since gone under, so I can republish here with clear conscience and under my own banner.

First appeared in Body Parts Magazine *as "Cannibal Society."*

Last Supper
More of a mood piece than anything else. I'm proud of the brutish efficacy of the first sentence, as well as the names "Corpumond" and "Ellisinae." They're meant to sound like something Gaiman would dream up, and I feel like I got pretty close.

First appeared in Liquid Imagination Magazine *as "Conspicuous Consumption."*

She's New in Town
A first chapter of a book that never materialized. I think it works rather well on its own. I'm quite fond of the physical characterizations here, and the small-town feel of the narration. I'd been reading a lot of Pollock recently, and I think it shows. This is a kind of *Knockemstiff* riff-on—with monsters and strange encounters in rainstorms alongside the hicks.

First appeared in Atlantis Literary Journal *as "Silver Circles."*

When It Rains
I'd just finished reading an anthology called *Meet Cute,* just a bunch of romance shorts about the moment couples meet for the first time. I set out to write the opposite: a story where a couple meets for the final time, again and again and again. This is probably the saddest thing I've ever tried to write, and I think it works even better coming off of "She's New in Town."

First appeared in The Crow's Quill, Quill & Crow Publishing.

Sometimes You Get Two
If "Song of the Summer" posits that the forces that drive people apart come from within us, then this story asserts the opposite: division comes from without, from the darkness, from evil forces beyond our control or comprehension. I don't know which version

of reality is the truth; I just know this was the story I had to write in 2021.

Original to this collection.

The Machete at the End of the World
Another "mood piece," combining two genres I'd never seen mashed together before: slashers and post-apocalyptic fiction. I began with the idea: What would Jason Voorhees do after the bombs fell? What does a killer do when there's nobody left to kill? I like to imagine this takes place in the same continuity as "Last Supper," and that the narrator would eventually discover the gourmands up on top of their building and butcher them the way they deserve.

Original to this collection.

About the Author

Don't buy the hype: Jacob Steven Mohr was *not* raised by wolves. Feral children are capable of many things, but weaving wild words into flesh 'n fantasy isn't one of them. Lucky us. If it were, we'd all be speaking Wolf. Mohr's work has appeared previously in *Night*

Terrors Vol. 20, *All Dark Places 3*, *Tales of Sley House 2021*, and *I Cast You Out!* This is his fourth book of fiction. Find him in Columbus, Ohio, or online @jacobstevenmohr.

Printed by BoD™in Norderstedt, Germany